THE FIRE AT
MARY ANNE'S HOUSE

**Other books by
Ann M. Martin**

P.S. Longer Letter Later
(written with Paula Danziger)
Leo the Magnificat
Rachel Parker, Kindergarten Show-off
Eleven Kids, One Summer
Ma and Pa Dracula
Yours Turly, Shirley
Ten Kids, No Pets
Slam Book
Just a Summer Romance
Missing Since Monday
With You and Without You
Me and Katie (the Pest)
Stage Fright
Inside Out
Bummer Summer

THE KIDS IN MS. COLMAN'S CLASS series
BABY-SITTERS LITTLE SISTER series
THE BABY-SITTERS CLUB mysteries
THE BABY-SITTERS CLUB series
CALIFORNIA DIARIES series

THE FIRE AT
MARY ANNE'S HOUSE

Ann M. Martin

AN
APPLE
PAPERBACK

SCHOLASTIC INC.
New York Toronto London Auckland Sydney
Mexico City New Delhi Hong Kong

Cover art by Hodges Soileau

ISBN 0-590-50390-1

12 11 10 9 8 7 6 5 4 3 2 1   9/9 0 1 2 3 4/0

Printed in the U.S.A.   40

First Scholastic printing, May 1999

*The author gratefully acknowledges
Ellen Miles
for her help in
preparing this manuscript.*

THE FIRE AT
MARY ANNE'S HOUSE

CHAPTER 1

"Tigger! You silly boy." I laughed as I moved Tigger one more time. I was lying on my bed, trying to do some serious reading. But my gray tiger-striped kitten, who can be a rascal when he wants to be, was more interested in playing games. He leaped upon each page as I turned it, pretending that the paper was a small animal and that he was a wild jungle cat after his prey.

"How am I ever going to learn about the 'Eleven Laws of Love,' or 'How to Make Him Yours Forever,' if you can't keep your paws off my magazine?" I asked Tigger.

Well, as you can see, my serious reading was actually not so serious. To be honest, I was leafing through the Hot Summer Fun issue of *Teenzine*, a magazine my dad calls "a monumental waste of time."

He's not totally wrong about that. I can't pretend that *Teenzine* is especially deep. But just then, it was exactly what I wanted to be reading. After all, it was a warm June afternoon. School had ended for the summer, and I was due for some relaxation. And even though my dad would probably prefer that I relaxed with more challenging reading material, I was sure he wouldn't deny that I deserved a little time to daydream. He knows I work hard, both in my classes and outside of school.

My dad's name is Richard Spier, and he's a lawyer. I'm Mary Anne Spier, and I'm not a lawyer. I'm just a thirteen-year-old native of Stoneybrook, Connecticut. I go to Stoneybrook Middle School (SMS), where I make above-average — but not perfect — grades. I have brown eyes and chin-length brown hair and I'm one of the shortest girls in the eighth grade. I'm not a supertrendy dresser (I'd never wear most of the wild stuff they show in *Teenzine*), but I do manage to look presentable. My style is preppy-but-casual. I like to look neat; no dreadlocks or huge baggy jeans for me. And my ears aren't even pierced, much less my nose or my belly button.

One of the models in *Teenzine* has, like, *everything* pierced. Plus, she has about six tattoos. Um, no thanks.

I think my dad is happy I turned out the way I did. He brought me up all by himself, since my mom died when I was just a baby. I don't remember her at all. Sometimes I stare at the pictures I have of her, hoping for some distant memory to pop into my brain. But that hasn't happened yet.

Anyway, my dad did his best to be both father and mother to me. And except for a brief time right after my mom died, when he was just too sad to cope and he sent me to live with my grandparents, he has always been up to the job. In fact, for awhile he tried a little *too* hard to be good at parenting. He was extremely strict. My friends couldn't believe how he controlled my life. He chose the clothes I wore (mostly little-girl dresses, even when I was in seventh grade), my hairstyle (braids, which went well with those dresses), and even my bedspread and posters (my room looked like an eight-year-old's). But as I matured and he loosened up a bit, he gave me more and more independence. I started to pick out my own clothes, do my hair the way I wanted, and decorate my room with things I'd picked out myself.

My dad's been fine with all my choices. (Who knows how he would react if I wanted to dye my hair pink, though!) He even approves of the fact that I have a boyfriend. Fortunately, Logan Bruno is the kind of boy any dad would like. He's polite and respectful and treats me *so* nicely. He's adorable too — not that my dad would care about that. Logan looks like Cam Geary, my favorite celebrity. They both have blue eyes, brownish-blond hair, and smiles to die for. Logan also happens to have this great Southern accent, left over from when he lived in Louisville, Kentucky.

There was a feature on Cam in *Teenzine*. I had already cut out the best picture — one in which he was playing with his dog on the beach — to add to my Cam Geary collage. Under the picture was a quote about how the dog was his best friend. It was so sweet it almost made me cry.

Don't tell Kristy I said that.

That's Kristy Thomas, my best friend from way back when. She's been known to give me a hard time about how sentimental I can be. Once, when we went to a sad movie together, she showed up lugging a huge box; it was a carton of Kleenex. That's her idea of a joke.

But I know Kristy appreciates how sensitive I can be. She always tells me what a good listener I am and comes to me for advice when she needs a sympathetic ear. And somehow, even though she's one of the most outgoing people on the planet, she understands and accepts the fact that I am one of the shyest.

Kristy is president of this club I belong to, the Baby-sitters Club (known as the BSC). Most of my friends belong too (even Logan). We all love kids and love sitting, so the club is a natural for us. I'll explain more about the BSC later.

First of all, though, I have to explain that my dad and I are now part of a much bigger family. One of the reasons Dad loosened up a bit as I grew older was that he was too busy falling in love to worry about my hairstyles.

Yes, love. It can even happen to grown-ups.

In this case, it was more like falling *back* in love, with an old flame . . . who happened to be the mother of my *other* best friend, Dawn Schafer.

Confused? I don't blame you. It's complicated.

See, back when he was a student at Stoneybrook High, my dad used to go out with this girl named Sharon Porter. But her parents didn't approve of the match. Eventually, she went to college in California, where she met and married a man named Jack Schafer. They had two kids, Dawn and Jeff. But the marriage didn't last, and Sharon ended up moving back to Stoneybrook with the children.

That's when Dawn and I met and became instant best friends. (Kristy had to adjust to sharing me, which she did. Dawn even became a member of the BSC.) Dawn is the greatest. She's a very relaxed person who never judges anyone or anything and who stands up for what she believes. I don't know if that's her upbringing or just the way she is. She's beautiful on the outside too, with long, straight, white-blonde hair and clear blue eyes. (It's obvious why her dad nicknamed her "Sunshine.")

Anyway, it didn't take long for us to figure out that her mom and my dad had been high school sweethearts. We fixed them up again, and soon wedding bells were ringing.

It was *so* romantic.

Dad, Tigger, and I moved into the house where Dawn and her mom were living. (Jeff had moved back to California by then, to live with his dad.) I *love* this house, and I already feel as if I've lived here all my life. It's an old, old farmhouse, with tons of interesting nooks and crannies, including a secret passage that Dawn believes is haunted. (I, myself, would rather not believe in ghosts. Too scary.) This house was actually a stop on the Underground Railroad! It's as if history is alive here. Sometimes I stare into the big brick fireplace and imagine all the people who have built fires there and warmed their hands at that hearth. Or, at bedtime, I'll climb the narrow stairway and picture some girl my age doing the same thing, carrying a candle to light her way. There's even a big old barn out back (it's connected by the secret passage), with bales of hay and old stalls, some with the nameplates for horses who once lived in them.

Anyway, there we were, one big happy family. Well, maybe not exactly that. It took us awhile to adjust to one another, to tell you the truth. For example, I love Sharon, but I have to say that she is just about the most disorganized person I've ever met. My dad, on the other hand, is Mr. Neat. His sock drawer is organized by color, with each pair neatly folded. Sharon doesn't even *have* a sock drawer, as far as I know. I've found her socks in the linen closet, in the china cabinet, and even — once — in the lettuce crisper in the fridge. (Don't ask . . .)

Also, Dawn and Sharon are both health food nuts who thrive on tofu. My dad and I, on the other hand, are omnivores. Our primary cookbook for years was *101 Fantastic Hamburger Recipes.*

Eventually, we ironed out our differences and settled into a happy blended-family life. But after some time, Dawn realized that she really missed California and that she wanted to live there again, like Jeff. It wasn't easy for us to let her go, but we didn't really have much of a choice. I know she's happier out there, even though she misses her Stoneybrook friends and family. And if she's happy, I'll try to be happy for her. I do miss her, though. More than I can say. And I know Sharon does too.

"Tigger!" My pesky kitten was at it again. I was trying to concentrate on an article called "Makeover Mojo," but Tigger insisted on being the center of attention. He lay down on the open magazine, rolled over onto his back, and purred as loudly as he could. That's his way of saying, "Pat my tummy."

I obeyed.

I didn't really mind. It wasn't as if I were trying to study for an algebra test or anything. If I didn't learn any new tips on applying eyeliner that afternoon, so be it. I'd survive. And I happen to enjoy patting Tigger's tummy.

But you know how cats are. Two seconds later, he'd decided it was time to head downstairs to see if there was any interesting food in his bowl. He jumped down from the bed and stalked off, twitching his tail. I plumped up my pillows, made myself comfortable, and went back to my reading.

I cringed through "Life's Most Embarrassing Moments" (I can hardly stand to read those — imagine having a visible booger in your nose the whole time you're talking to your principal), skimmed over "Backstage with U4Me" (I don't care that much about what a rock band does between sets), and checked my horoscope to see if anything wonderful was going to happen in the next few days (nope). Finally, I flipped to the back page to check out the Contest of the Month. I've never entered a *Teenzine* contest, since they're usually pretty dumb. Last month's was about who could come up with the best name for a new deodorant. Can you imagine wasting your time thinking about that?

But this month's contest was different.

"Hey, neat!" I said out loud as I read the headline. Finally, a contest I could care about. "Baby-sitter of the Year," it said. "Who's the coolest, most together baby-sitter you know? Is it you? Your sister? Your best friend? Write and tell us all about her — or him. Contest winners will be featured in our back-to-school issue!"

The headline was followed by a long list of rules and guidelines. I pored over them. Could one of the BSC members win this contest?

Absolutely. No question about it.

I glanced at the clock on my bedside table. It was 5:10, almost time for me to leave for that afternoon's BSC meeting. I shoved the magazine into my backpack and headed to the barn to grab my bike.

I could hardly wait to tell my friends the news.

9

CHAPTER 2

One of us was sure to win . . . but who? I thought about this as I rode over to Claudia's house. Each and every member of the BSC is an excellent example of what a baby-sitter should be. How were we going to figure out which one of us should enter the contest?

Maybe I should explain a bit more about the club. The BSC meets three times a week, Monday, Wednesday, and Friday afternoons from five-thirty to six. We always meet at Claudia Kishi's house — in her room, to be exact. We've been together as a club for quite awhile; in fact, sometimes I have a hard time remembering that we haven't *always* been a club. We've grown and changed over time, but the basic idea of the club has been the same. We provide responsible, excellent baby-sitting services to our clients. That's it.

How does it work? Well, our clients call us during meeting times to set up jobs. (That's the genius part; the parents only have to call one number to reach a whole group of sitters.) In the beginning we had to advertise, but now we have plenty of regular clients. We schedule jobs according to which sitters are free at which times (we even have two associate members — Logan, and a girl named Shannon Kilbourne — to lend a hand when the regular members are booked solid).

We make sure to arrive on time to our jobs and to come prepared, which may mean bringing our Kid-Kits (special boxes we've decorated and filled with toys, games, markers, and stickers) on a rainy day. We keep track of what's going on with our clients by writing up every job in our club notebook.

Who came up with all of these brilliant ideas for making the BSC work so well? My best friend, Kristy, that's who. Which is why she's president. Still, the club is a success because of *all* the members. Each of us contributes something different and special. That's why it was so hard for me to figure out which member should enter the contest.

If I were going to nominate Kristy for Baby-sitter of the Year, for example, it would be because of the energy and enthusiasm she has for everything she does.

Kristy is a whirlwind. Her life is busy and chaotic, but she flies through it with ease. She seems to thrive on having too much to do. She's part of a huge family, she runs the BSC, and she also manages a softball team for little kids.

Meeting Kristy's family for the first time would be overwhelming for anyone. (*Living* in it would be overwhelming for me!) She has two older brothers, Charlie and Sam, plus one younger one named David Michael. Kristy's dad walked out on the family when David Michael was a baby, leaving Kristy's mom to cope with raising four kids on her own. But surprise! Kristy's mom is one tough cookie. She not only managed, she did a great job. And then she won the Excellent Husband sweep-stakes when she met and married Watson Brewer, one of the nicest grown-ups I know. He came complete with two kids of his own from his first marriage, Karen and Andrew. They live with Kristy's family part-time, in Watson's ultragigantic mansion. (Oh, did I forget to mention that Watson's a millionaire?) Kristy also has a new younger sister, Emily Michelle. She was a Vietnamese orphan whom Kristy's mom and Watson adopted soon after they married. And then there's Nannie, Kristy's ex-tremely cool grandmother, who came to live with them as well.

Could the house be any more packed?

Well, yes, as a matter of fact. I haven't even

begun to list the pets, which include one huge puppy, one feisty kitten, some goldfish, and an ever-changing cast of smaller pets that travel back and forth with Karen and Andrew.

All I can say is that it's a good thing Kristy has all that energy. She needs it.

Not that the rest of us are slouches. Take Claudia. She's the BSC's vice-president, mainly because we meet in her room. (We meet there because she's the only member with her own phone line.) Claudia is hardly a couch potato. She's a wildly creative person who lives for art. And to Claudia, everything is art — from paintings hanging in museums to the way a person does her hair.

I could nominate Claudia for Baby-sitter of the Year because she brings her creative spirit to everything she does, including caring for children. Our charges just love her.

Claudia is Japanese-American, with long, glossy black hair. She lives with her parents (Mr. Kishi is an investment banker, Mrs. Kishi is a librarian) and her older sister, Janine, who is truly brilliant, at least in an academic way. Janine has no artistic talent whatsoever. (Claudia, on the other hand, does not do all that well in school. She's smart, but she isn't fulfilled by learning algebra equations and spelling rules.)

As vice-president, Claudia has no real duties other than taking phone calls for the club during nonmeeting times. But she has designated herself our official Provider of Munchies and makes sure to have plenty of yummy snacks on hand for every meeting. It's a job she enjoys because she is a junk food junkie. She hides the stuff in her room, along with her Nancy Drew mysteries, since her parents don't approve of them either.

Claudia always makes sure to have some sugar-free snacks on hand for her best friend, Stacey McGill. Stacey is diabetic and has to be extremely careful about what she eats. In case you don't know, diabetes is a disease that prevents the body from properly processing sugars. In order to stay healthy Stacey has to give herself daily injections of insulin, a hormone her body doesn't produce. Diabetes is a lifelong problem, but Stacey has learned to live with it. Looking at her, you'd never know what she's had to go through. She seems extremely healthy, with her bouncy blonde hair and bright blue eyes.

I'd base Stacey's nomination for Baby-sitter of the Year on her gift for organization. As the BSC's treasurer, she keeps track of all the money we earn. She also collects dues each week, which we use to help pay Claudia's phone bill, for buying markers for our Kid-Kits, and so forth. She always knows how much we've saved — to the penny.

Stacey grew up in New York City. Her dad still lives there, but since her parents divorced, Stacey and her mom have lived in Stoneybrook. Stacey visits her dad as often as possible. She still loves the city, partly because of all the shopping opportunities there. Stacey is into fashion. She has an extremely sophisticated style. You'd never mistake her for someone who grew up in a small town.

We have another ex-New Yorker in the club: Abby Stevenson. Abby and her twin sister, Anna, grew up on Long Island and only moved to Stoneybrook recently. Their mom works in publishing and commutes into Manhattan on the train. Mr. Stevenson died in a car accident a few years ago, when Abby and Anna were nine.

Maybe you would expect Abby to be a sad person because of that. And underneath, I think she is very sad. But the face Abby shows to the world is anything but. She has an outrageous sense of humor and loves to keep people laughing. In fact, I'd nominate her for Babysitter of the Year just because she's so much fun. And what kid doesn't love to laugh?

Abby has nearly as much energy as Kristy. She channels most of her intensity into sports. Abby is a super athlete. I wouldn't be surprised to see her in the Olympics someday, playing soccer or running the one-hundred-yard dash. The amazing thing is that she does it all even though she's constantly battling allergies and asthma, two problems that can make it hard for her to breathe.

When Abby and Anna first moved here, we invited both of them to join the club. Anna declined, saying she was too busy with her music (she's an outstanding violin player). Abby's way busy too, but somehow she manages to fit in a few sitting jobs here and there.

Their interests may be different, but the sisters do look alike. Both have dark curly hair (though Anna's is short and Abby's is long), and both wear contacts or glasses. Still, we rarely mix them up. Once you know them, it's hard to mistake one for the other.

Like everyone else I've told you about, Anna and Abby are thirteen (they recently celebrated their Bat Mitzvahs, a ceremony for Jewish girls coming of age). But there are two members of the BSC who are younger, Jessica and Mallory. Both of them are eleven and in the sixth grade, and while they're only allowed to sit in the afternoons (or for their own families at night), they are both just as responsible as the rest of us.

Jessi Ramsey is the most graceful person in our school, if not our whole town. She's strong and athletic too. That's because she's been studying ballet since she was little. She's such a good dancer that she was invited to New York not long ago to take part in a workshop with a real ballet company. Jessi brings her sense of grace and strength to everything she does, including baby-sitting, which is why she could be Baby-sitter of the Year. Jessi has a baby brother named Squirt (well, his real name is John Philip Ramsey, Jr.), and a younger sister named Becca. Both her parents work, and her aunt Cecelia lives with the family and helps take care of the kids.

Mallory Pike, Jessi's best friend, comes from a much larger family. She has seven brothers and sisters! Mal has reddish-brown hair and freckles, and she wears glasses. She wants to be an author/illustrator of children's books someday, and she writes all the time. She is the only BSC member who truly enjoys writing up jobs in the club notebook. Maybe her natural talent for documenting the changes that our charges go through would be enough to win her the Baby-sitter of the Year award. Mal hasn't been sitting too much lately, though, since she has been away at a boarding school called River-bend. That's why she's now an honorary member of the BSC, while Jessi's a junior officer.

"Mary Anne! Earth to Mary Anne!"

Oops. I was so involved in thinking about my friends' baby-sitting talents that I almost rode my bike right past Claudia's house. Fortunately, Kristy and Abby were just hopping out of Charlie's car (Kristy's brother drives them to meetings in his old clunker, the Junk Bucket).

"Hey!" I said, putting on the brakes. I got off my bike and joined them. As we walked up the stairs to Claudia's room, I filled Abby and Kristy in on the contest, showing them the page from *Teenzine* with all the rules on it. I knew I should wait until the meeting started, but I was too excited. "The thing is," I told them, "I can't figure out which one of us should enter. We all have our strong points."

Once everyone was settled in Claudia's room (Stacey and Jessi arrived soon after we did), Kristy called the meeting to order. Then we started talking about the contest again. I explained that I'd already figured out why each of them should be nominated.

"What about you?" Kristy asked.

I hadn't thought about that.

Stacey smiled at me. "I think Mary Anne should be nominated because she's so caring. Isn't that a great quality for a sitter to have?"

"I second that," cried Kristy.

"I third it," added Abby.

I blushed and felt like crying. "Thanks, you guys," I said. "But really, how do we decide which one of us should enter?"

"We don't," said Kristy.

"What do you mean?" I asked.

She held up the page of rules, which she'd been studying. "We enter as a group!" she said. "There's nothing in here that says we can't."

"Cool!" yelled Claudia. She reached under her bed for a bag of pretzels and began passing them around. "Let's start celebrating now because we are definitely going to win."

Everybody cracked up. But you know what? I had a feeling Claudia was right. Add it all together: energy and enthusiasm + creativity + organization + caring + a sense of fun + grace and strength + a knack for keeping track of things. Together, we're an incredible combination. What single baby-sitter could beat us?

CHAPTER 3

Thursday

Why we like to baby-sit.
1) We like kids.
2) Baby-sitting is fun. Usually.
Unless the kids are really cranky
or if something bad happens, like
a charge breaks his arm.
3) ~~We like kids.~~

"Aughh!" Kristy groaned and ripped the page off the pad. She crumpled it up and threw it into Claudia's wastebasket. "Score! Two points," she yelled.

I glanced at the overflowing wastebasket. "You've made enough points to win the World Series all on your own," I told her.

"The World Series is baseball," Kristy reminded me patiently.

Claud was sitting at her easel, sketching Kristy and me as we worked. It was Thursday, and we were at Claud's house, where we'd been looking through the BSC notebooks and records, in order to start work on our contest entry.

Teenzine was not making it easy for us. If we wanted to be named Baby-sitters of the Year, we were going to have to work for it. The contest rules were demanding. Each entry had to have three parts: a history of the entrant's baby-sitting experiences, "testimonials" from charges, and an essay on why the entrant likes to baby-sit. Not only that, but we had a very tight deadline to meet. The entry had to be postmarked by next Tuesday.

Kristy was working on the essay. Without much luck.

"Why should this be so hard?" she asked with a sigh. "Why should it be hard at all? I love baby-sitting — we all do — but I can't figure out how to explain *why*."

"Have you tried making an outline?" I suggested.

She shot me an exasperated Look. "I've tried everything."

I couldn't help giggling. "We've only been here for half an hour, Kristy," I pointed out. "Don't give up yet." I held up my pad, which was blank. "I haven't even started writing yet," I confessed.

At the meeting the day before, I'd been nominated to work on the history part of the entry. Mal would have been perfect for the job, but her school doesn't end for another week and a half, so I was stuck with it. Actually, I didn't mind so much. It was fun to read through all the old notebook entries.

But I was beginning to realize that my job might be a real challenge. There was just so much to choose from! The BSC has had so many experiences. I'd have to write a whole book — a whole *set* of books — if I wanted to tell our complete story. But did I have time for that? No way. Instead, I'd have to pick out some of the highlights and concentrate on them.

If some Hollywood producers ever got to know

Jackie Rodowsky, they could make a million bucks with a movie about that kid. Of course, they'd need to hire a stuntman (stuntboy?) to do the things that Jackie does in real life. But The Jackie Rodowsky Story would be full of thrills, chills, and suspense. Will Jackie survive another fall down the stairs? Will Jackie be able to put together the lamp he broke before his mom gets home? Will Jackie's baby-sitter have a nervous breakdown? The tale of Jackie, the Walking Disaster, will be coming soon to a theater near you.

I couldn't help laughing as I read that entry, written by Dawn when she still lived here. We've all had the Jackie Rodowsky experience. He's an adorable seven-year-old who is so accident-prone he should probably be walking around in full body armor.

"What's so funny?" asked Claudia.

"Oh, just some stuff about Jackie," I said. I read it out loud. "Has anybody ever sat for him when he *didn't* break something — either a bone in his body or a window or —"

"Or his head," said Kristy grimly. I knew she

was remembering a time Jackie had hurt himself seriously. He'd been riding his bike without a helmet, and he smashed into a tree. He ended up in the hospital with a concussion.

Kristy was shaking her head. "That's not one of my favorite memories," she said. "Thank goodness he was okay."

"We've had some close calls," I said, remembering a few scary times. "How about when Jenny had that high, high fever?" I shuddered just thinking about it. Jenny Prezzioso is four. Once when I was sitting with her, her temperature soared to 104 and she had to be taken to the hospital. It turned out she had strep throat.

"You handled that well, though," said Kristy. She smiled at me. "But you're not just going to write about all the disasters, are you? What about the funny stuff?"

"There must be plenty of that," Claudia chimed in.

"There is," I said. "Hold on a second." I flipped through the notebook. Then I laughed. "Do either of you remember what a googleblaster is? Or a snorkaphone?"

Kristy looked bewildered, but Claudia cracked up. "I do," she said. "Those are both instruments. The kids were going to have an orchestra. I remember when Stacey and I helped the Barrett-DeWitt kids make theirs."

"That's just what I was reading about," I said.

Hey, Claud, here's a riddle for you: What do you get when you take 7 kids, add 3 boxes of Kleenex, 4 toilet paper tubes, 2 oatmeal boxes, and 3 balls of string?

I don't know, Stacey, what do you git?

Well, you sure don't get an orchestra. But you do get one wild night at the Barrett-DeWitts....

Orchestras, parades, circuses . . . The BSC has helped with so many fun events. The kids we sit for come up with the wildest ideas. And some of the sweetest ones too. Like the time Charlotte Johanssen, a nine-year-old we sit for regularly, thought of making Thanksgiving food baskets for the residents of Stoneybrook Manor, a retirement home in town. All the kids were excited about it, especially Buddy Barrett. He could hardly wait for the first basket-making meeting, according to Jessi's entry in the notebook.

I was scheduled to sit for the Barretts on Tuesday, so when I called to find out if it was all right to bring them to the meeting, Buddy was ecstatic. Not about the meeting, but about where it was going to be held....

25

"Where was the meeting?" Kristy asked, curious. I'd been reading aloud again.

"Take a guess," I said, smiling.

"In your barn," chorused Kristy and Claudia.

All the kids love to do stuff in my barn. I think it has to do with the hayloft, and the way you can play hide-and-seek in the horse stalls. It's especially nice in there on rainy days, when the comforting smells of the barn make you feel all cozy and safe. Plus, there's the secret passage.

"Remember when we were positive there was a ghost in the secret passage?" I asked the others.

"I still think there is," said Claudia.

"Even after we discovered the truth about those noises?" Kristy asked.

Nicky Pike, one of Mallory's younger brothers, gave us a real fright one time when he hid out in the secret passage — partly because we thought he was lost, and partly because of all the creaks and weird sounds we'd heard coming from there. "I'll have to include that episode in our history, for sure," I said, making a note.

"What about the time when Jake was missing?" said Kristy. "Don't forget to put that story in."

How could I forget? Jake Kuhn, who's only eight, was gone much longer than Nicky (Nicky was only missing for a few hours). Jake disappeared for two days, while everyone in Stoneybrook searched for him. "Matt was a real hero that day," I said. Jake had finally been found — he'd fallen through the cellar of a house under construction — by Matt Braddock, a seven-year-old who's profoundly deaf.

"Yikes," said Claudia, shaking her head. "That was so scary. Let's go back to some of the funny memories!"

"Gladly," I said, leafing through the notebook. "How about the time Jessi sat for the Mancusis?"

Kristy laughed. "I knew that was going to be trouble!"

The Mancusis don't have any kids. So why did they need a sitter? For their menagerie of pets! Jessi volunteered and ended up with a missing snake, runaway dogs, and a sick hamster, who turned out to be pregnant.

Maybe it wasn't so funny at the time, but it is now. That's true of a lot of BSC moments, I guess. Like the time we sat for twenty-one (Count them! Twenty-one!) children. That was when Kristy came up with the brilliant idea for Mother's Day Off, when the BSC members treated all our clients to a free day of sitting. There weren't any great disasters, and we sure made the mothers happy, but it was a wild day just the same.

I made a few more notes:

The time Jake was lost
Jessi at Mancusis'
Mother's Day Off

Then I sighed. It was going to take forever to write up the history. If only Mal were here to help.

From the other side of the room, Kristy sighed too. "If it weren't for the incredible publicity we'll get from winning this contest, I'd give up now," she confessed. She crumpled another piece of paper and tossed it into the wastebasket.

Claudia looked from my discouraged face to Kristy's. Then she grinned. "I had a feeling you guys might need a little extra boost at some point," she said. "Wait just a second." She ran downstairs and came back a few minutes later carrying a plate piled high with fudge brownies that she'd baked just for us. "You know what I always say," she told us. "No matter what the question is, chocolate is the answer!" (Plus nachos for Stacey!)

As usual, when it comes to junk food, Claudia is right. After a couple of brownies, Kristy and I felt a lot better. By the end of the afternoon, we still hadn't gotten very far with our contest entry, but we had sure had fun reminiscing.

CHAPTER 4

Thursday

Well, I must say it feels good to be appreciated. Even when the appreciation is shown in... well, strange ways. Charlotte was thrilled to help me gather testimonials from our charges, but wait until you guys see (and hear) the bizarro collection of endorsements we ended up with. I wonder if the other contestants will be submitting references like these.

Little did we know. While Kristy and I were struggling with our parts of the contest application, Stacey was keeping busy too, collecting testimonials from our charges.

Stacey was sitting for Charlotte Johanssen that afternoon. I should mention that she and Charlotte are very close. In fact, they call each other "almost sisters." Since neither has any siblings, they share a special bond. Stacey is the older sister Charlotte never had, and Charlotte is the younger sister Stacey always wanted.

Charlotte adores Stacey and is also a big BSC fan in general. So when Stacey mentioned the Baby-sitter of the Year contest that afternoon, Charlotte jumped on the idea.

"Baby-sitter of the Year!" she said. "That's you, Stacey. You're the Baby-sitter of the *Decade*. You're the Baby-sitter of *Forever*!"

Stacey laughed. "That's sweet, Char. And you're the Charge of Forever. But I'm not entering this contest on my own. The BSC is entering it as a group."

"That's even better," said Charlotte. "Because if you won, the others might feel jealous. This way you'll all win."

"Well, maybe," Stacey said. "It's always possible that there's some other baby-sitter out there who might deserve to win more than we do."

"No *way*!" Charlotte shouted.

Stacey laughed.

"So what do you have to do for the contest?" Charlotte asked.

"Three things," answered Stacey, ticking them off on her fingers. "We have to put together a history of our baby-sitting experiences, write an essay on why we like to baby-sit, and collect some testimonials from the kids we sit for."

Charlotte looked confused. "What's a testimonial again? I think I know, but not really."

"It's when somebody says how great you are," said Stacey. "Sort of like those detergent ads, when the mom goes on and on about how well the soap removed stains from Jimmy's jeans?"

"Or in the magazines, when they have all those quotes from people about how much weight they lost using some dumb diet system?" Charlotte asked.

Charlotte is one smart kid.

"Exactly," Stacey said.

"I can write you one!" cried Charlotte, jumping up. They'd been sitting on the porch, enjoying the afternoon sun. She ran inside and came back a few seconds later with a pad and a pencil. As Stacey watched, amused, Charlotte began to scribble away. A few minutes later, she signed her name with a flourish at the bottom of the page. "Done!" she said. "Want to read it?"

"Sure," Stacey replied. "Or maybe you'd like to read it to me."

"Okay." Charlotte picked up the pad, cleared her throat, and began to read. " 'The BSC is the best. They are all the greatest baby-sitters in the universe. I would never want any other baby-sitters but them, and if my mom hired one I would hide under my bed until she went away.' "

Stacey stifled a giggle. Charlotte continued to read. " 'I have been baby-sat by every member of the BSC: Kristy, Claudia, Jessi, Mary Anne, Mallory, Stacey, Abby, and Dawn. Even Logan and Shannon have been my baby-sitters. I swear that they are all the most excellent sitters, especially Stacey, who is the — ' " she paused. "Is there such a word as 'excellentest'?"

Stacey shook her head, smiling.

"I didn't think so," said Charlotte. She made some quick corrections, then finished reading. " '. . . especially Stacey, who is even more excellent than the rest.' " She looked up. "That's it! Then I signed my name. Do you think this will help you guys win?"

"Definitely," said Stacey. "No question about it."

"But you'll need more, won't you?" asked Charlotte.

"We'll need a lot," Stacey answered.

"Well, what are we waiting for?" Charlotte jumped up again. "Let's go!"

"Wait," said Stacey. "You mean you want to go around collecting written testimonials?"

"Why not?" Then Charlotte stopped to think. "Hmm," she said. "Not all the kids you sit for are old enough to know how to write. Hold on a second." She dashed into the house and returned a few minutes later, carrying her backpack. She showed Stacey what she had inside. "Remember when I was — you know — spying a little?" she asked, blushing slightly.

Stacey remembered. Charlotte and some of the other charges we sit for had gone through a big spying phase after reading *Harriet the Spy*. It had caused more than one fight among friends, and we BSC members had been relieved when the kids eventually grew tired of spying on one another.

Charlotte had hoped to avoid the problem Harriet ran into (having her secret spy notebook stolen and read) by using a tape recorder instead. Her plan hadn't worked, but Charlotte still had the tape recorder. "This will be perfect," she told Stacey. "We can record what kids have to say and send the tape as part of your contest entry."

"Sounds like you have a plan," said Stacey, allowing herself to be swept up by Charlotte's enthusiasm.

Charlotte ended up recording several "testimonials" that afternoon, interviewing kids from her neighborhood as well as a few others she and Stacey found at the playground. She did an excellent job too. But will we send the tape along with our contest entry? Stacey wasn't sure it would be a good idea, unless we added a few explanations. And when the rest of us heard the tape, we had to agree.

"My name is Becca Ramsey, and I'm eight years old. My favorite baby-sitters are the coolest baby-sitters on the planet. They always let me stay up as late as I want. They let me watch really scary movies. And I can eat anything in the fridge. My baby-sitters rule!"

"The BSC? They're great. Every time I break my arm or a finger or something they know just what to do. They're always there, ready to help bandage a cut or sew my pants or glue together a vase or something. Oh. My name is Jackie Rodowsky, and I'm seven."

"I'm Norman Hill. I'm seven. The BSC members are excellent. Last time Kristy sat for me she didn't give me a single cookie, even though I was begging her for one. She gave me carrot sticks instead."

"I'm Adam Pike. I'm ten. How much are you going to pay me to say the BSC sitters are the best?"

"Jordan Pike. Also ten. Or would you rather pay us to not tell how bad the BSC stinks?"

"We'll say whatever you want. But we'll need — let's see — three dollars and seventy-nine cents. Oh. I'm Byron. Ten years old."

Eek!

Charlotte collected several other testimonials that day, but most of them were just as strange as the first ones. We couldn't send in a tape like that without making sure the contest judges understood a few things.

For example, Becca misunderstood Charlotte's question. She thought it was a game in which you said what your *fantasy* Baby-sitters of the Year would be like. And Charlotte was in too much of a hurry to tape it over.

Jackie — well, that's Jackie. If you didn't know better, you'd think we were the most irresponsible sitters in the world. I mean, if we were watching, our charges wouldn't hurt themselves in the first place, right? And how were the contest judges to know that Jackie can't go a whole day without breaking something, no matter who's watching him?

Norman Hill? He's a great kid, but even he admits that he's overweight. He's always trying to diet. He says it helps when we baby-sitters keep him away from temptations.

And the Pike triplets don't always sound like gangsters trying to extort money. It's just that they're obsessed with saving up enough for this "really awesome" model plane they saw at a store downtown.

As Stacey said later, we know our charges love us, and we know we're good baby-sitters. But she wasn't sure that Charlotte's tape was going to get that across to the contest judges. We were going to have to keep working on those testimonials.

CHAPTER 5

If only I had known.

But what if I had? What would I have done differently? Would it really have helped to know in advance that my life was about to change so suddenly and dramatically?

Friday was a day like any other. There wasn't anything special about it, not really. But it was the last normal day I was going to have for a long, long time.

Maybe that's what I would have done differently. Maybe I would have tried to savor Friday for what it was: normal and uneventful. The kind of day you don't appreciate until something terrible comes along.

It's like when you come down with some miserable, sneezy, stuffed-up, runny-nose, bad-cough cold. Once you feel well again, you're so happy just to feel okay. Breathing normally feels like the best thing in the world. You're grateful for your health. But pretty soon you start taking your good health for granted again — at least, until the next cold comes along.

Does that make sense? I hope so. Anyway, bear with me while I tell you about my Friday. My normal, uneventful Friday. The last day I took my life for granted.

I woke up at around eight-thirty. Isn't summer the greatest? I love not having to set an alarm. I like to wake up whenever I've had enough sleep, feeling rested and ready for the day. I stretched and yawned, and Tigger, who was sleeping on the foot of my bed, stretched and yawned too. Then he padded across the quilt to give me one of his gentle little kitty-kisses, on the tip of my nose.

"Morning, Tigger," I said.

He purred as I rubbed his head. He loves to have his head rubbed first thing in the morning.

I looked around my room, enjoying the way the morning sunshine lit up the white lacy curtains hanging at the windows. Sharon and I had been talking about painting my room later in the summer; I was thinking about yellow, but I hadn't decided exactly what *kind* of yellow. I squinted at the walls, trying to imagine a soft buttercup shade. Or what about a more golden yellow, like an egg yolk?

Suddenly, my stomach rumbled. "I'm hungry," I told Tigger. "Bet you are too."

A few minutes later, I headed downstairs, dressed in my favorite old bathrobe. It's red plaid flannel, so old that it's almost falling apart. I'd hate to be seen in it by anyone but family, but it's so soft and cozy I can't seem to throw it away. Tigger thumped down the stairs ahead of me, meowing hungrily.

"Is that a wild jungle cat I hear?" my dad said as I came into the kitchen. "And his brave tamer?"

I laughed as I kissed his cheek. "Morning, Dad." My dad was obviously in a good mood. Sharon, on the other hand, was not. She was looking glumly into her mug of herbal tea, and she barely looked up when I kissed the top of her head. "Morning, Sharon."

"Oh, good morning, sweetie," she said, snapping out of her funk for a moment. "Sleep well?"

I nodded. "How about you?" I asked. I knew Sharon hadn't been sleeping well lately.

She shook her head. "I woke up at three and couldn't fall asleep again for the longest time," she said. "I just lay there, worrying about how I was going to find time to do this report Marjorie needs by Monday."

Sharon works for a woman who has her own small accounting business. Lately Sharon doesn't seem too happy with this job. I don't think she finds the work all that interesting.

Also, Sharon works really hard, but I don't think Marjorie appreciates her.

My dad gave her a concerned glance. "I didn't know you were awake," he said. He patted her hand. "Poor you."

"Poor me," agreed Sharon with a smile. She shrugged. "Oh, well." She took one last sip of her tea. "Time to hit the road."

My dad stood up. "Time for me to go too," he said. "See you tonight, ladies." He put his mug in the sink, kissed Sharon and me in turn, and grabbed his briefcase. Then he was out the door.

Sharon left a few minutes later, after the usual frantic search for her car keys (she never leaves them in the same place twice — this time they were in the silverware drawer). "See you tonight, sweetie," she called as she left.

I fed Tigger, then settled down at the table with a bowl of cereal and the latest L.L. Bean catalog. I was hoping to find the perfect pair of shorts — not too long, not too short — to wear through the summer.

After breakfast, I did the dishes. Then I headed back upstairs to make my bed and get dressed. I was in the midst of tidying up my room when the phone rang. I ran out and picked up the extension in the hall.

It was Logan. "Good morning," he said.

"You're up early," I told him. Logan often

sleeps until eleven or so on summer mornings.

"That's because I wanted to catch you before you ran off to some sitting job," he said.

"No job today," I reported.

"Great! Then how about a picnic?"

What a terrific idea. "I'd love to," I said. "What should I make?"

"Nothing," said Logan. "My mom wants me to use up some leftovers. There's potato salad and coleslaw and stuff for sandwiches. I'll bring everything over to your house and then we can decide where to go."

It sounded wonderful. Unfortunately, by noon the sun had disappeared and a light rain was beginning to fall.

"Bummer," said Logan when his mom dropped him off. "I wanted to go over to Miller's Park."

"We'll go there another time," I promised. "Today we're going to dine in style." I led him into the barn, where I'd laid out a red-checkered tablecloth over a couple of planks balanced on two sawhorses. I'd set my make-shift table with napkins and paper cups and I'd brought out a big pitcher of homemade lemonade.

"This is excellent," Logan told me. He unpacked the food and we had a feast. Afterward we took turns jumping into the hay, something I hadn't done for years. One of the things I like best about Logan is that I can act like a little kid around him. I don't have to pretend I'm somebody I'm not. He likes me just the way I am.

When Logan left (okay, okay, I'm leaving out the part when he kissed me in the hayloft), I put away the picnic things and spent a little time working on the Baby-sitter of the Year contest entry. Then I took the book I've been reading (*My Side of the Mountain*, for the third time) onto the porch. I lay there in the hammock, feeling cozy as the rain dripped off the eaves. I read and napped for the rest of the afternoon.

Summer rules, doesn't it?

By late afternoon it had stopped raining, so I rode my bike over to Claudia's for the BSC meeting. We had a lot of fun that afternoon. Stacey brought over the tape Charlotte had made, and we listened to the "testimonials" and laughed so hard our stomachs hurt. Our charges may mean well, but they make us sound like the meanest, most irresponsible sitters on earth!

After Stacey played the tape, Claudia passed out Twizzlers and Reese's peanut butter cups. (She had Frookwiches for Stacey, cookies sweetened with fruit juice instead of sugar.) Then Kristy asked us for help with the essay she was working on for the contest.

"I just can't seem to find the right way to start," she said. "I don't know if I should be funny or serious. Should I list all the reasons we like to sit? Or should I give examples? What *are* all the reasons we like to sit?"

We sat there, munching our snacks and thinking.

Kristy looked desperate. "I have to have this done by Monday," she reminded us. "Come on, you guys."

"This is too much like homework," Claudia said. "This is supposed to be our summer vacation, isn't it?"

"Too bad Mal's not here," Jessi said. "She'd enjoy a job like this."

"I can't think of a thing," said Abby. "I mean, besides the obvious stuff. And I'm sure you've already thought of all that."

"Anyway, it's six o'clock," Stacey pointed out. "Meeting's over."

"Augh!" Kristy was frustrated. "All right. I'll do it myself. But just remember who to thank when we win the contest!"

When I arrived home, my dad and Sharon were already there. Dad was mowing the lawn, and Sharon was rummaging around in the fridge, trying to find something for dinner. She looked tired and not much happier than she'd looked in the morning.

"How about if I make my special spaghetti?"

I suggested. It was the least I could do, after I'd had such a nice, relaxing day.

Sharon gave me a grateful look. "Would you?" she asked. "That would be heaven." She kissed me, grabbed the newspaper, and went into the living room.

I bustled around in the kitchen. I'm not a great cook, but there's one thing I can make, and that's spaghetti. I use sauce from a jar, but I add stuff to it (the recipe is a secret!) to make it extra tasty. I threw together a salad too. Then I set the table and called Dad and Sharon in for dinner.

As we ate, I tried to ask Sharon about her day at work, but she dodged my questions. She just didn't seem to want to talk about her job. My dad, on the other hand, gave us a blow-by-boring-blow account of this case he was working on, something to do with a property dispute between neighbors. Sharon and I listened politely, but I'm sure if you asked either of us to tell you the details afterward, we wouldn't have been able to.

After dinner, Sharon thanked me and went off to work on her report. Dad headed into the living room to watch a news show, and I went upstairs to call Dawn.

We talked for half an hour or so, about nothing in particular. I told Dawn about the contest the BSC was entering, and she told me about a movie she'd seen. It's always good to catch up with my favorite (and only) stepsister.

After I hung up, I watched TV with my dad for awhile. Then I headed for bed, along with Tigger and my book. I read for a few minutes, then turned off the light and went to sleep.

And that was my normal, uneventful Friday. Not a very special day, but one I'll never forget.

Hours later, I woke up. Something was tickling my nose. Tigger! He was walking around on my pillow, making little meowing noises. Sleepily, I glanced at the clock. It was 4:42. In the morning. Why was Tigger waking me up now?

Then I heard it. A regular, high-pitched, shrieking sound. I remembered it from the day, months ago, when my dad had been checking the fire alarms in our house.

Fire alarms?

I sat up in bed.

CHAPTER 6

Tigger's meowing grew louder as soon as he saw that I was awake. He leaped off the bed and ran toward the door, which was closed. Then he ran back to me and meowed some more.

The shrieking noise didn't stop.

But now I could hear something else.

"Mary Anne! Mary Anne, wake up!"

It was my father's voice, from down the hall.

I was awake, there was no doubt about that. Totally and completely awake.

And terrified.

I didn't think — I *couldn't* think. I grabbed Tigger in my arms, swung my legs over the side of the bed, stood up, and walked toward the door.

"Mary Anne!" my father's voice was closer now.

Even though I was awake, I felt as if I were in a dream. Everything was happening so fast

— but at the same time, I felt as if I were moving in slow motion. Don't ask me to explain how that could be. It just was.

Tigger struggled in my arms, but I tightened my grasp on him. Then I reached out with one hand to touch the door before I opened it.

Why?

To see if it was hot.

Somehow, I remembered that from all those lectures during Fire Prevention Week at school every fall. "Don't open a door without checking first to see if it's hot. The fire may be raging on the other side."

Fire.

My house was on fire. It couldn't be happening, but it was. That's why Tigger was behaving oddly. That's why my dad was shouting for me. That's why the alarm was shrieking.

I could smell smoke now.

And I could hear odd sounds. Cracks and pops coming from the other side of my door.

"Hurry!" my dad cried.

The door felt warm but not hot. I opened it a crack — and smoke billowed into my face. I stepped back.

Then a hand reached in and grabbed my wrist. My dad. "Let's go!" he said. "Sharon's already downstairs, probably outside. We have to get out. Now!"

He pulled me along through the smoke-filled

hall and then made me start down the stairs in front of him. The temperature seemed to rise ten degrees for every step we went down. Smoke filled the air. Dark, hot, horrible-smelling smoke. I tried not to breathe it in, but there was no way to avoid it. Clutching Tigger, I stumbled down the stairs with my dad behind me.

I still couldn't see flames, but I sensed that they were near. The alarm hadn't stopped shrieking. It was going on and on, penetrating my brain. The heat was almost unbearable now, and the smoke made it hard to see. I was coughing and choking as I reached the bottom of the staircase. The front door was only yards away. If we could make it there, we'd be safe.

"Drop and roll!" my dad yelled in my ear.

Another phrase from fire prevention lectures.

I didn't stop to think. I did as he said. I dropped to the floor and rolled, clutching Tigger to my chest. It was cooler on the floor and a little less smoky. I could breathe without choking.

"We're almost at the door!" yelled my dad. "Stay down!"

I wasn't about to argue. Besides, I'm not sure I could have stood up if I'd tried. Holding Tigger more tightly with one arm, I crawled along the floor.

Tigger had stopped squirming by then. I

guess he sensed, somehow, that I would take care of him.

"Richard! Mary Anne!" I heard Sharon shouting. Her voice sounded very close. If she was outside, that meant we were almost there too. The smoke was so thick by now that it was hard to see the front door.

But suddenly, I caught a momentary breath of fresh air. The door! It must be standing open. I pulled myself along, ignoring the pain in my knees as I desperately crawled forward. I felt in front of me for the doorframe, waving a hand wildly until I touched wood. I grabbed it and pulled myself up and out.

Then I was on the porch. The heat of the fire poured out of the open door behind me.

I felt a hand on my back. "Run, now," my father shouted. "Run!"

"This way!" cried Sharon. "Oh, Mary Anne." She was sobbing as I ran into her arms. "You're safe. You're safe. Oh, Richard!"

We stood in a little knot beneath the apple tree in our front yard, holding one another as tightly as we could. It came to me then that the apple tree was the place we'd agreed to meet long ago, when we'd made an escape plan in case of a fire. I still hadn't let go of Tigger, but he didn't seem to mind being squished among the three of us. My dad and I gasped for breath. I couldn't stop coughing.

Then I heard sirens. "I called for help," Sharon said through her sobs. We broke apart, and she looked down at her hand, which held our white cordless phone, the one from the hall table. "I guess I must have grabbed the phone on my way down the stairs," she said wonderingly.

"Good thing," said my dad. "The house is going fast."

I didn't want to look, but at the same time I had to. I had to see what was happening. Slowly, I turned around.

What I saw was so awful I don't think I'll ever be able to forget it. My house — my *home* — was burning. Huge orange flames shot out of the kitchen window, and smoke billowed through the open front door. I could see flames licking at the staircase I had just come down. There was a roaring sound, and crackling, and occasional loud bangs. The flames grew larger as I watched, and they began to boil out of the dining room window as well. The fire looked like a living thing, a hungry, destructive thing that was devouring my house.

The bright flames stood out against the night sky. There were no lamps on in the house since we'd all been asleep, so the only light came from the fire. I held Tigger close as I watched the flames spread. He still wasn't struggling.

And then the fire trucks arrived. Sirens wailing, lights flashing, they pulled into our yard. Three trucks, one right after another. Firefighters dressed in long coats, high boots, and helmets leaped off the trucks and began to pull hoses toward the house.

"Stand back, please. You'll need to stand back," said a tall man in a helmet that said CHIEF. "Is everyone out?"

My dad nodded.

"Was anybody hurt?"

My dad shook his head.

"Good," said the chief.

"My papers — " began my father.

The chief shook his head. "You can't go back in. Not now. We'll do everything we can to save your house."

Sharon's sobs grew louder. "My purse!" she cried. "My pictures! Why didn't I grab everything?" My dad put an arm around her shoulders and pulled her close.

"It's good that you didn't, ma'am," the chief told her. "Your safety is the most important thing." A voice crackled over the radio he held. He listened, then spoke quietly into it. "I'm needed now," he said. "You folks stay right here. Don't move. And whatever you do, don't even think about going into that house. I'll make sure someone keeps you up to speed on what's happening."

Then he was gone.

I thought: *Go into the house? Is he out of his mind?* I couldn't imagine taking one step closer to it. By now flames were coming out of all the windows on one side of the house. The roar sounded like a freight train, the crackling noises were louder, and sparks flew up into the night air. I could feel a wall of heat as the fire blazed on.

Sharon couldn't stop crying.

I hadn't started.

I, who tear up at the sight of a puppy. Who dissolve into sobs while watching commercials. Who know every scrap of dialogue from *Titanic* and *Roman Holiday*, the two saddest movies ever made.

I didn't cry.

I couldn't cry.

Not one tear.

I just stood there, watching as the firefighters swarmed over the house, working to save it.

I suppose I was in shock.

I saw a woman approach Sharon and hug her. Mrs. Prezzioso, from down the road. She was wearing a purple bathrobe. I remember thinking that the color looked good on her.

Then Mr. and Mrs. Braddock appeared, and Mr. Pike. People hugged me, and I hugged them back without thinking. By that time, the whole neighborhood must have been awake. If the sirens hadn't woken people, the noise and heat and light from the fire would have.

Sharon was still crying. My dad, like me, was just staring at the house. Then a firefighter approached our group. "Which one of you is the homeowner?" he asked. My dad stepped forward.

"I am," he said. "Or, rather, we are." He held out an arm toward Sharon. She leaned into him.

"Okay," said the firefighter. "Here's the thing. We're going to have to do some demolition in order to try to save part of the house. We'll be chopping up through the second floor, before it collapses. We'll also be breaking windows, to let out the heat and smoke and gases. We may have to break through the roof too. Chief wants you to understand what's happening."

My dad nodded.

"Any questions?" the firefighter asked.

My dad just shook his head. I guess he was in shock too. Sharon blew her nose into a handkerchief someone had handed her. She was still crying too hard to speak.

Then Mrs. Prezzioso stepped forward. "I'm just wondering if there's any danger to other houses in the neighborhood," she said. "I mean, should I be getting my daughters out of bed?"

"Good question," said the firefighter, looking

around at the gathering of neighbors. "At this point, we're working to contain the fire. We're hoping to keep it confined to this house, and right now it looks as if we may be able to save the barn. Fortunately, there's not much wind tonight, so the fire isn't spreading as fast as it could. So far, no other houses are in danger. But we'll make sure to let you know if that changes at all."

Mrs. Prezzioso nodded. "Thank you," she said. Then she stepped back to Sharon's side and put a hand on her shoulder.

I felt a hand on my own shoulder and turned to see who it was. Stacey was standing there.

"Oh, Mary Anne," she said. Her face was white. "I'm so glad you're safe."

I nodded slowly. I was glad too.

"Mom says you should come to our house. You don't have to watch this."

I shook my head. "I'm staying," I said. My voice sounded like a croak. Those were the first words I'd said since Tigger woke me up.

I had to stay. I had to find out if any part of my life could be saved.

CHAPTER 7

I watched for a long time, even though I could hardly stand to look. I knew it was a fact that my house was burning down, but I still couldn't believe it. It just didn't seem real.

The heat and flames continued for a long time. More fire trucks arrived, and firefighters ran all over the house and yard, shouting and gesturing as they took their positions. Their figures were silhouettes of black against the brilliant orange flames that continued to pour out of the house.

Some of the firefighters wore oxygen tanks strapped to their backs and masks that made them look like scuba divers. They disappeared into the heat and noise, carrying axes and powerful flashlights. Others knelt or stood, holding hoses in both hands as they sprayed huge arcs of water into windows and through the doors. There was even a firefighter way up high, on a ladder attached to one of the trucks. He sprayed from above, trying to put out the flames that were rising from the top of the roof.

When water hit the flames, black smoke would billow skyward. The fire would die down for a moment, then spring up again in another spot nearby.

I saw the staircase inside the open front door, now completely engulfed in flames. I saw the outline of ceiling beams as the fire ate through the dining room. I saw a whole wall fall outward and crash, sending up a volcano of sparks.

The fire was so powerful it took my breath away. It seemed to shrug off the efforts of all the people trying to stop it.

And then, finally, it began to lose ground. The water was winning. Now there was more smoke than flame, and the heat was less intense. But I couldn't stop watching.

"Mary Anne, do you want me to stay here with you?" That was Stacey. She had come and gone a few times during the time I stood there watching. Once she'd put a coat over my shoulders and brought me a backpack with a change of clothes. Another time she brought me a sandwich and a bottle of water. Her mom had made a whole stack of sandwiches for the firefighters and for me, Sharon, and Richard.

I hadn't touched the food. "No," I answered dully.

Stacey hugged me, and I let her. "Then I'm going home to sleep for awhile," she said. "Do you want to come to my house?"

I shook my head. She hugged me again, and when she stepped back I saw tears in her eyes. "Thank you," I croaked. "Thank you, Stacey." Then she left, and I turned back to look at the house. The sky was turning light behind it, to the east. Through the smoke I could see a pinkish glow to the clouds high above the blackened wreckage.

Tigger was still with me. I had finally put him down, but he hadn't wandered off. He was staying close by, weaving around my ankles and meowing anxiously. I knew he must be upset by what was happening.

Sometime later — I don't know how long, but I know that the sun was all the way up by then — a firefighter talked with my dad and Sharon. "It's dying out," he said, waving a hand toward the fire. There was still a lot of smoke, and parts of the house were still smoldering. But it was clear that he was right. The fire was dying out.

I felt that I was dying out too. I couldn't even start to think about what it meant to lose my house, to lose everything *in* my house.

To lose everything.

"It'll still be awhile before we can let you any closer," the firefighter told us. "Once the fire is

57

really out, we'll make sure the scene is safe. The inspectors will need to do some investigating too. They'll try to figure out where the fire started and why."

My dad just nodded. He looked exhausted. His face was pale, and there were black circles under his eyes. Sharon's eyes were puffy and red. She had stopped crying, and now she just looked dazed.

"We'll need to make some calls," said my dad. He held up the portable phone Sharon had brought out of the house. "I guess this isn't going to work anymore," he added with an odd little laugh.

I pictured the base of the phone, on the hall table upstairs. Only, the hall table probably wasn't there anymore. I wasn't even sure if there was an "upstairs" anymore.

Mrs. Prezzioso overheard my father. "I brought you the cell phone from my car," she said, handing it to him. "I thought you might need it. Keep it as long as you like." She gave each of us a quick hug. "I have to head home," she said. "But please, let me know if there's anything I can do to help." She glanced at the house and back at the three of us. Her eyes were filled with tears. Then she walked off.

My dad watched her go. "Let's see, who do we have to call?" he asked, thinking out loud. "I'll make a list." He stopped to pat his chest, where his shirt pocket — complete with pen — would normally be. My dad's a big list maker, and usually carries a pen and a little notebook wherever he goes. But his pajama top didn't have a pocket.

I looked from Sharon to my dad and then down at myself. The three of us were standing there in our p.j.s, and suddenly that seemed kind of funny. I was wearing a pink nightgown printed with 50s-style illustrations of kittens playing with a ball of string. Sharon had on a holey old green T-shirt of my dad's and a pair of those boxer shorts they make for women in gray cotton. Over that, she'd thrown an old peacoat a neighbor had brought. And my dad was dressed in red plaid pajamas, matching tops and bottoms, of course. Neighbors had also brought us random socks and shoes.

I almost laughed — until I realized something. The nightgown I was wearing was the only piece of my own clothing I still had. Even my old red plaid bathrobe was gone now. I twisted the ring on my finger — my mom's ring from when she was my age.

Suddenly, it wasn't so funny anymore.

It wasn't funny at all.

"Don't you keep a notebook and pen in the car?" Sharon asked.

"Of course," said my dad. He turned to look at the two cars — his and Sharon's — parked along the side of the driveway. "Good thing neither of us parked nearer to the house last night," he said.

"Good thing we have a wide driveway, so the fire trucks could pull in," added Sharon.

I couldn't think of any good things to chime in with. It all seemed pretty rotten to me.

My dad went off to his car and came back with a pad and pen. "I also found the phone number for our insurance agent," he reported. "It was on my car insurance card. I suppose that's one of the calls I should make first." He began to make his list.

I couldn't believe how organized he was. I couldn't even begin to think about what to do next.

After he'd finished the list, my dad and Sharon began to take turns making calls. First Dad called the insurance agent. Then Sharon called her parents, who I know as Granny and Pop-Pop (that's what Dawn calls them). They still live in Stoneybrook, over on Bertrand Drive. I knew they'd be upset to hear about the fire. And I knew Sharon would urge them to stay home, since Pop-Pop has a heart condition.

After Sharon hung up, Dad asked me if I wanted to call anyone. I shook my head, so he took the phone and called his boss. Then Sharon called hers.

Next, Dad called Grandma Baker, in Iowa. She's my mother's mother, but my dad has become closer to her in recent years. And since neither of his parents is living, I guess he wanted to speak with her. He asked me if I wanted to talk to her too but I just couldn't. When he hung up, he told me that she had sent me all her love.

Sharon sighed. "I think it's time to call Dawn and Jeff," she said. "I hate to wake them up with this news, but they have to know sometime."

Dawn. It was the first time I'd thought of her. How was she going to feel? She had lived in that house, and I knew she loved it too.

Sharon talked to Jack and Carol first and told them a little about what had happened. (Carol is Dawn's stepmother.) Then Carol woke Dawn first and put her on the phone. I could tell by listening to Sharon's half of the conversation that Dawn was shocked and saddened.

"She wants to talk to you," said Sharon, holding out the phone.

My first impulse was to say no. I wasn't ready to talk. But it was Dawn. How could I refuse? I took the phone. "Hi," I said.

"I thought you'd be crying," Dawn said. I could hear that she was. She kept sniffing.

"Not so far," I said. "I'm just — I don't know. I can't really talk yet."

"I can understand that. Listen. I'm going to catch the first plane I can. I want to be there with you."

I nodded. Then I remembered she couldn't see me. "Good," I said. "That's good." I couldn't think of anything else to say, so Dawn and I said good-bye and I handed the phone back to Sharon. She spoke to Dawn again, and then to Jeff, who must have woken up by then. I could tell he was asking if he could come with Dawn. Sharon gently told him she thought it would be better if he stayed in California for the time being. I knew she thought the fire would be too upsetting for someone his age.

When she hung up, she hugged me. "That's from Dawn. She made me promise to give you a big hug."

The hug felt good. Any other time, that hug would have brought on my tears. But my eyes stayed dry.

A few minutes later, I heard car doors slamming, and Kristy ran up to us, with Watson and her mom right behind her. She hugged me, hard. "Oh, *man!*" she said, staring at the house. "It's really true. Stacey just called to tell me, and we came over as soon as we could."

I followed her eyes. The house — well, it wasn't a house anymore, really. It was a pile of blackened wood. The brick chimney still stood, and two walls, but that was about it. The whole mess just lay there, smoking.

Watson shook his head. "I'm so sorry," he said. Kristy's mom hugged Sharon.

"Guess what?" Kristy asked me. "Watson had a great idea."

"We'd like you to come and stay at our place," Watson said to us. "For as long as you need to. We have plenty of room, and we'd love to have you. I know you can't think too far into the future right now, but there's no doubt you will need a place to live for awhile."

I hadn't even thought of that, but it was true. I saw my dad and Sharon look at each other. "My folks' house isn't nearly big enough for us," Sharon murmured. My dad nodded.

"We accept," he said. "That's extremely generous of you."

"Yea!" Kristy yelled. Then she must have realized how that sounded. "I mean, I wish you didn't have to come. But I'm glad you will."

Just then, Stacey came back into the yard, followed by Claudia, Logan, Abby, and Jessi. My friends. They gathered around me with hugs and kind words. It was good to see their faces, but somehow having them there made the situation seem even weirder. It was as if their presence meant I had to start believing that my house really had burned down, but I couldn't quite do that. I still felt as if I were having a dream. A nightmare. Only I knew I was wide awake.

I saw the fire chief approach our group. "The fire is pretty much out now," he said. "It'll still be some time before we're done here, but you can go a little closer if you want. So far, it appears that the fire was caused by some faulty wiring in the kitchen. We'll have a full report on that soon."

My dad and the fire chief talked a bit longer. Then I moved closer to the smoldering pile to take a look.

The house — *my* house — was totally gone.

CHAPTER 8

"This was my study," my dad said in a strange, strangled voice. "Right here. My desk was by that window, and my files — " He stopped and moaned. *"My files,"* he repeated.

The firefighter who was standing next to him nodded. "It'll be awhile before you can take it all in," she said sympathetically.

It was a few hours later. My friends had left, all except Kristy. (Everyone else had offered to stay, but I told them I'd call them when I knew how they could help.) Kristy's mom had taken Tigger back to their house to settle him in. We'd been sitting on the grass, talking, when the fire chief approached my dad and Sharon.

"I wish we had been able to save more," he said. "But these old buildings — "

"I understand," Dad said. "We certainly appreciate all that you did. I hope you'll pass on our thanks to your crew."

"I'll be sure to. Now, there will be some salvageable items in the house," he went on. "But they'll take some finding. In some places, where the second floor fell in, things on the first floor will be pretty well buried."

"When can we start looking?" asked Sharon.

"Anytime now," said the chief. "I'll assign a couple of firefighters to escort you in, at least for the first few times. It can be dangerous in there, even when the fire is totally out." He gestured toward the house.

I didn't doubt it could be dangerous. It looked horrible. The house was nothing but a huge pile of rubble, all blackened and soaked with water.

"Maybe you'd like to start with the barn," suggested the chief. "There was very little fire damage in there, although there was smoke and water damage to the outside."

We looked at the barn. It was hard to believe it was still standing. I thought of how much fun Logan and I had had jumping into the hay. Had that really been only yesterday?

It felt like years ago.

"It's amazing you were able to save it," my dad said. "And I do want to check it out. But I think I'm eager to head into the house and see what we can find."

Sharon nodded. "I feel the same way."

I wasn't so sure.

The chief spoke into his radio, asking for two

volunteers to escort us inside. A few minutes later, a short blonde woman who introduced herself as Pat showed up. "Eric's coming too," she told the chief. While we waited for him, Pat asked us friendly questions about things such as how long we'd lived in Stoneybrook. My dad answered them. I still wasn't interested in talking to anyone.

Soon, Eric, a tall African-American fire-fighter, appeared. "We checked and it's safe now to approach. Are you folks ready to check things out in there?" he asked, nodding toward the house.

My dad and Sharon said they were.

I felt like screaming, "No! I'm not ready and I don't know if I ever will be!" But did I?

No way.

I stood up and followed the others. Feeling numb, I walked toward the house. Kristy followed me.

We didn't have to walk up the porch stairs; the porch was pretty much flattened. And the front door was nothing but a splintered frame. Pat led the way through it as Eric stood back, waiting for us to pass. Two of the outer walls still stood — the one facing front and the one on the left. The back wall and the one on the right, where the kitchen had been, were gone. The ceiling was gone too, at least where my room had been. Sharon and Dad's room didn't exist anymore either. Nor did the attic. That ceiling had fallen in too. The corner of the house where Dawn's room was, the one nearest to the barn, still stood. That meant that the secret passage might still be there.

The floor was covered with wet, blackened debris — pieces of the ceiling, chunks of wood, partially burned objects I couldn't identify. I had to watch every step I took. Pat and Eric led the way, pointing out the gaping holes in the floor.

There was a terrible blend of smells in the air. It didn't smell like the nice kind of fire you have in your fireplace. Most of the smells were completely unfamiliar. There was one like burned rubber — maybe from the upholstered chairs? — and one like a huge wet dog. That must have been from all the water the firefighters had poured onto the house.

I stood in the middle of what used to be the living room and looked up. With the second floor and the attic gone, and the roof torn open, I could see straight up to blue sky.

It was the strangest feeling.

"Wow," breathed Kristy. She was standing next to me, staring upward. "That is so weird."

"You never get used to it either." That was Pat, who was standing nearby. Her firefighter's coat was hanging open, her hair was falling out of its ponytail, and her face was smudged with soot. She looked exhausted.

"This is where the couch was," Sharon said in a bewildered voice. She had picked her way through the debris covering the living room floor and was staring at a spot in front of her. A bulging lump on the ground with a couple of springs poking out of it looked as if it might once have been a couch. She waved a hand around. "And the TV was over there, and the bookshelves — " Her voice broke. "The book-shelves," she repeated. "All my favorite books. And the pictures of Dawn and Jeff." She put her face in her hands and I could tell that she was crying again.

My dad found his way to her and put an arm around her shoulders. "This won't be easy," I heard him say. "But we'll get through it."

Sharon nodded. "Go ahead and check your study," she told him. "I know you want to see what's left."

"If anything," he said grimly. He gave her one more hug and then headed toward his study, which is — or rather, used to be — off the living room. I headed that way too, and so did Pat.

My dad looked devastated as he glanced around at what was left of the room. "I — I just can't believe it," he said. "How can all of this be here one moment and gone the next?" He shook his head. "I never should have kept my files here. They would have been safer at the office."

"Maybe," said Pat. "But a fire can strike any-where."

My dad started poking through some of the piles of debris on the floor. "Maybe I can salvage some things," he said. "Maybe some of my computer disks will still be readable."

Pat frowned. "I hate to tell you, but disks melt even before paper burns. Do you have files backed up on your office computer by any chance?"

My dad brightened a bit. "Actually, I do. Not everything, but a lot." Then his face fell. "But I've still lost so much." He looked over at me with a little smile. "Remember that pencil holder you made for me when you were in kindergarten? I still had that on my desk. I never found anything I liked better than that tin can covered with macaroni pieces."

I tried to smile back at him. "I'll make you another one," I wanted to say. But the words wouldn't come out.

"Well." My dad sighed. "I guess I can spend some more time in here later. We should probably look over the rest of the house first."

Pat agreed. Eric and Sharon joined us as we picked our way into the kitchen, which was in even worse shape than the rest of the house. There was really nothing left in there except for the burned-out shells of the refrigerator, stove, dishwasher, and sink. There were more gross smells in the kitchen, smells I couldn't identify. I thought of all the delicious smells there had been in that room over time. My dad's waffles. Sharon's vegetable stir-fry. A pan of brownies. The kitchen had been the center of our home, and now it was gone. Just gone.

"These old kitchens," murmured Pat. "I've seen it happen before. The wiring just isn't set up for all the appliances we use nowadays."

"We had it checked — " my dad began.

"I'm sure it was up to code," said Eric. "But things can still go wrong." He shrugged. "The investigators may be able to tell you exactly what happened, depending on what they find."

Sharon reached out to touch the stove. "It's still warm," she said. "The stove feels as if I'd just been cooking on it." She turned to look around her. "All my spices," she said. "My cookbooks. I've had some of those since college."

It was overwhelming. How could we begin to remember everything that we'd lost? Think about it. Close your eyes and try to picture every single thing in your kitchen. The boxes of cereal. The pictures on the walls. The clock.

The coffee machine. The can opener. Hundreds of other items — maybe thousands!

And that's just the kitchen.

"Cookbooks can be replaced," my dad said, hugging her. "Remember, the important thing is that we're all safe. None of us was hurt. That's all that matters."

He kept saying that, but I wasn't convinced. Somehow, even though none of us had been hurt, I felt as if someone or something had died.

I looked down into a pile of charred junk and saw something glinting. I bent to pick it up. A fork. It was covered in soot and sort of bent, but I recognized it as one of our forks. One of the ones my dad and I had brought to this house when we moved in. It might have even been the fork I had eaten dinner with the night before. I handed it to Sharon. She took it, tears rolling down her face.

We moved through the house, looking at what was left. The bathtub. The fireplace (funny, huh?). Two toilets. Piles and piles of junk that we would have to dig through.

"I left my wedding ring on the bedside table," Sharon told Pat at one point. "Do you think there's any chance I'll find it?"

"You never know," Pat said. "The strangest things can turn up when you start shoveling. One woman found her son's bronzed baby shoes at the bottom of a huge pile of debris."

I thought of the things that were most precious to me. My journal. My pictures. The small cedar box where I keep letters and certain sentimental things such as ticket stubs from movie dates with Logan. I could see now that I wasn't likely to find any of it.

Suddenly, I felt too tired to stand. Kristy must have noticed. "Want to come back to my house for awhile?" she asked.

I shook my head. I wanted to keep searching. But Sharon and my dad, who had overheard Kristy, insisted.

"You go on and get some sleep," Dad told me. "You need your rest." He hugged me, and so did Sharon.

Then I let Kristy lead me away.

CHAPTER 9

Saturday

Jessi, you're a genius!

Oh, shucks. I'm blushing.

No, I mean it. The kids were really feeling scared, but our visit downtown took care of their fears.

I think you're right. It was fun too, wasn't it?

Totally. I'm going to bring all the kids I sit for. They're going to love Sparky.

Who's Sparky? Good question. He's a dog, a dalmatian. And he's the Pike kids' new best friend.

Abby and Jessi didn't know anything about Sparky when they arrived to sit for the Pikes on Saturday morning. All they knew was that as soon as they'd heard about the fire, Mr. and Mrs. Pike had called Claudia's number to arrange for a sitter so they could go to my house and help out. Claudia had called around to see who was free and Abby and Jessi ended up with the job. They were volunteering their time as a way of helping my family.

By the time they arrived, every one of the Pike kids had heard about the fire. The interesting thing, Jessi told me later, was how each of them was dealing with the news. "All of them were upset," she told me, "and they were really worried about you and relieved to know that you were all right. But beyond that, they each had their own way of coping."

"Jessi, Jessi, have you seen Mary Anne yet?" asked Claire, the youngest Pike (she's five). She threw herself into Jessi's arms when she and Abby walked into the dining room, where the Pike kids were finishing up a late breakfast. "Is she really okay? Really? The fire didn't burn her?"

"She's fine," Jessi told her. "I saw her a little while ago. She's just fine."

"Is she going to have to move away from Stoneybrook now?" Claire asked worriedly.

"No way!" said Jessi. "Of course not." She and Abby found seats at the table and settled in to answer more questions.

"But what about her house?" asked Margo (who's seven). She was pushing a half-eaten pancake around on her plate. "What about Tigger? What about all her things?"

"Her house — " Jessi didn't know exactly what to say about that. "She won't be able to live in her house for awhile," she explained finally. "She and her dad and stepmom are going to stay at Kristy's, did you know that?"

Margo nodded. "What about Tigger? Is he okay?"

"He's fine," Jessi assured her. "He'll be with Mary Anne at Kristy's."

"But what about all her clothes and her favorite things?" asked Margo. "What about them?"

Abby spoke up. "A lot of Mary Anne's things were burned up," she said matter-of-factly. "But that's not important. What's important is that Mary Anne and her family are okay."

Margo didn't look convinced. "I know it's good that they're safe," she said. "But if it was me, if my house was on fire, I would try to grab all my favorite things, like my shell from Sea City, and my best Beanie Babies, and — "

"You can't do that," Abby interrupted. "Fire is very dangerous. If there's a fire in your house, the most important thing is to get out."

"I know," Margo admitted. "Mom and Dad taught us about that. We know what to do."

"Stop, drop, and roll!" yelled ten-year-old Jordan, one of the triplets. He waved his fork around, scattering drops of maple syrup. "That's what you do if your clothes catch fire."

"We learned that at Fire Prevention Day," said Adam (another of the triplets), "when they burned that car out on the recreation field. Remember? That was so cool." He stuffed an entire small pancake into his mouth and chewed noisily.

"But I bet the fire at Mary Anne's house was way cooler," said Jordan. "I heard the flames were, like, a hundred feet high. And you could feel the heat a couple of blocks away."

"And six fire trucks were there," said Adam enthusiastically, swallowing his gigantic bite of pancake. "Even a ladder truck. That is so cool."

Byron, the third triplet, was a little less swept up in the excitement. He tends to be more fearful than the other two. "How did the fire start?" he asked. "Was somebody playing with matches?" His plate was still stacked with pancakes. He didn't seem to have much of an appetite.

"I don't think that was it," answered Abby. "But you're right that playing with matches is really dangerous. So far the fire department thinks the fire at Mary Anne's had to do with something in the electrical system."

Byron nodded. He still looked worried. "How did they know when the fire started?" he asked.

"I guess it was because the fire alarms went off," Abby told him. "Fortunately, Mr. Spier is one of those people who follows all the directions about keeping your alarms' batteries fresh."

"I'm going to tell Dad to check ours," said Byron.

Adam and Jordan were still excitedly comparing notes on things they'd heard about the fire. "It took hours to put it out," said Adam.

"I heard that one of the firefighters was almost hit by a falling beam," said Jordan. "Those guys are so brave!"

"I might want to be a firefighter when I grow up," put in Nicky, whose face was smeared with the raspberry jam he prefers on his pancakes. He's eight.

"I used to think that," said Adam. "Like, when I was in first grade. I thought it would be so cool to turn on the siren. But there's a lot more to it than that."

"I know," Nicky said defensively. "It's not just the siren part."

But Abby had a feeling that the siren was, actually, what attracted Nicky the most. "How about sliding down the pole?" she asked.

"Yeah!" Nicky's eyes lit up. "I always wanted to do that. And then they have their boots waiting at the bottom of the pole. They jump into those high boots and pull up their firefighter pants all at the same time. I saw it on a video."

"I can't believe the way you guys are talking," Vanessa said. "It's like all you care about is how cool everything is. What about Mary Anne? What about the tragedy of her life?" She held up a pad on which she'd been scribbling. Her plate of pancakes was untouched. "I've started a poem about it. I think it's going to be really good too. It's going to make everybody who reads it cry."

Vanessa, who's nine, wants to be a poet when she grows up. She's known for creating epic poems for every occasion. Her siblings are sometimes a little impatient with the ones that go on for more than two pages.

"I'd like to hear your poem when it's done," Jessi told Vanessa, reaching out to pat her hand. "I bet it will be wonderful."

Soon, Abby and Jessi could see that breakfast was over, so they organized a cleanup. With all the kids helping, it didn't take long. At one point, when the kids were busy loading the dishwasher, Jessi pulled Abby aside and whispered an idea to her. Then she slipped off to make a phone call.

"Guess what?" she asked the kids when she came back to the room. The kitchen was now tidy and everything had been put away. "I know about a little field trip we could go on."

"Where?" asked Claire.

"To the fire station!" Jessi told her. "I just called and asked if we could drop by, and they said they'd be glad to see us."

Jessi had noticed how the news of the fire at my house was affecting the kids. She figured a trip to the fire station would give them a chance to talk about their fears and learn some rules about fire safety. She'd remembered hearing that the fire department welcomed visitors anytime. Sure enough, when she'd called to explain the situation, the firefighters on duty had been happy to invite them to drop by.

"Really?" asked Nicky.

"Cool!" Adam yelled.

"When can we go?" Claire looked eager.

"Right now," said Jessi. "They're waiting for us."

And so they were. By the time Jessi and

Abby and the Pikes arrived at the station (it's quite a walk), the firefighters were set for visitors.

"Come on in, come on in," said a big man who introduced himself as Mike. The kids walked into the station, looking around with interest at the trucks, the equipment, and the racks of coats. "The crew just finished cleaning our trucks," Mike told us. Sure enough, they were shiny and bright, gleaming as if they were brand-new. "That's one of our big jobs, keeping our equipment clean and in working order."

He introduced a couple of other firefighters, including a man who was on phone duty. Then he began a tour of the firehouse. He showed the kids where the firefighters cooked and ate and slept, and explained how they had to be ready at a moment's notice if a fire was reported.

"Then you slide down the pole, right?" Nicky asked eagerly.

"Unfortunately, we don't have a pole here." Mike sighed. "We have to use the stairs."

Nicky looked disappointed.

"We run down pretty fast," Mike continued, "and jump into our boots. Want to try on a pair of boots?"

"Yeah!" Nicky's face lit up. The other kids were excited too. Mike led them all through the firehouse, letting them try on not only boots but the heavyweight coats and pants the firefighters wear. He showed them how an oxygen mask works and let them try one on.

"We can't let you try on our hats because they're too heavy for young heads," Mike explained. "But here are some hats you can have for keeps." He handed out red plastic firefighter helmets that said FIRE CHIEF on them. Jessi wondered for a second if the kids would think the helmets were babyish, but they accepted them happily.

Mike handed out pamphlets too. "Ten Tips for Fire Safety," said one. It told about installing smoke detectors, making a fire escape plan, and other things families can do. He even had a pamphlet for Jessi and Abby called "Fire Safety Tips for Baby-sitters."

Then he let the kids climb all over the truck and showed Nicky where the switch was for the siren. "That's the best part of being a fireman," Abby heard Mike confide.

Just as the kids were finishing their tour, Abby heard barking. "That's Sparky," said Mike. "One of the other guys took him home last night. I'm glad he's back." A door opened, and a wriggling, happy dalmatian ran in to greet Mike. The kids gathered around.

"Can we pet him?" asked Margo.

"You sure can," answered Mike. "But it's

good that you asked. You should always check with the owner before you pet a dog you don't know." Sparky turned out to be a sweet, friendly dog, according to Jessi and Abby. He loved the attention the kids gave him.

By the time Abby and Jessi rounded up their charges for the trip home, they could tell that the Pike kids were feeling a lot less worried and scared about the fire at my house.

The field trip had been a success.

CHAPTER 10

"Mmmph," I muttered as I stretched and rolled over. *Why* was I so tired? Maybe because I'd been having horrible dreams about sirens and lights and blazing fires.

I rubbed my eyes and opened them — and the strangest feeling washed over me. Where was I? Pink curtains, striped wallpaper — this wasn't my room.

Then I remembered.

It wasn't my room because my room didn't exist anymore.

The sirens and lights and blazing fires hadn't been a dream.

My house had burned down.

For a moment, I wanted to shut my eyes again, pull the blanket over my head, and forget.

Forget about the fire.

Forget about everything that had been lost.

Forget about the fact that my whole life had changed overnight.

But there wasn't much point in that. After all, no matter how hard I pretended, the facts were the facts. I wasn't waking up in my own familiar room after a good night's sleep. I was waking up in one of the guest rooms at Kristy's house after a couple of hours of sleep. I had to stop and think to remember what day it was — Saturday — and to figure out that it must now be late afternoon.

I had tumbled into bed the second we arrived at Kristy's, without taking a shower or even washing my face. My hair still smelled smoky, and so did my nightgown.

I heard a light tapping on my door.

"Mary Anne?"

It was Kristy.

It took all my energy just to say, "Come in."

She entered and sat on the bed. She looked into my face. "How *are* you?" she asked quietly.

Wow. Kristy was being, well, different than usual. The Kristy I know would have barged into my room and started yakking away. This Kristy was gentle and cautious. It was almost weird. I felt the way hospital patients must feel when their long-lost relatives start trooping into their rooms. When Uncle Stan shows up, you know it must be serious.

"I'm okay," I said. "I mean — "

"I know," she said in a quiet voice, laying a hand on mine. "You're totally *not* okay, but what else is there to say?"

I stared at her. Where had this new, sensitive Kristy come from?

"What?" she asked, flashing a sudden grin. "I'm just trying to act the way you would act if our roles were switched."

We know each other so well.

"Well, stop it," I demanded. "You're scaring me."

"Okay," she said, jumping to her feet. "So, do you want something to eat? Do you want some clothes to wear? Who should I call to meet us at your house? I was thinking we could arrange shifts, so that you always have someone there to help you go through stuff. Also, I've already spoken to the rest of the club members about taking over any jobs you were signed up for. And Abby's going to be the secretary for awhile, so you don't have to think about that — "

I held up a hand. "Thanks, Kristy," I said. It was good to know that at least *one* thing hadn't changed. My best friend was still herself.

A little later, after I'd dressed in the clothes

Kristy had loaned me, she and I headed back to my house.

Or should I say to the spot where my house used to be?

A whole crew of people was there. Some were picking through the debris while others were sorting salvageable items that had been laid on a big tarp on the lawn. Mrs. Prezzioso was there, and Kristy's mom, and Mr. and Mrs. Pike. Granny had showed up, even though Sharon had urged her to stay home with Pop-Pop. My dad and Sharon were still trying to dig through layers of blackened junk, hoping to find things such as her framed portrait of her great-great-grandfather, who had come to the U.S. on a boat from Ireland.

Both of them looked exhausted. Sharon's face was smudged with soot; my dad's hands were filthy. "Hi, sweetheart," Sharon greeted me. She smiled and held up her left hand. "Look what I found!"

"Your wedding ring! That's great," I said. I made an effort to smile at her. I was finding it a little easier to talk. But it was still hard to grasp the enormity of what had happened. Sharon and I were standing in the middle of what had been the dining room — but I only knew that because the bottom of the staircase, mostly burned but still standing, helped me figure out where I was.

Our dining room table was gone.

So were the chairs with the tapestry seats.

The china cabinets, and their contents, no longer existed. No more big platters to be used on holidays. No more crystal wineglasses, the ones I'd drunk sparkling cider from, toasting the New Year with Dawn. No more silver pitcher —

"Look!" Sharon exclaimed. She'd been digging frantically in one spot, unearthing layers of what had once been the second floor in order to reach a much lower layer. "Don't you think this must have been that silver pitcher?"

I looked at the misshapen, lumpy, blackened object in her hand. "I don't know," I said. But I did know. It *was* the pitcher. I just wished she hadn't found it at all. It was harder to see it ruined.

Kristy nudged my elbow then. "Want some help?" she asked.

I had told Kristy I wanted to try to find some things from my room. I didn't expect to be able to save much, but I wanted *something*. Something from my past, something that would prove to me that my past existed.

"Sure," I told her. We left Sharon to her digging and walked to the other side of the almost-destroyed staircase. I looked up. It was still unnerving to see the sky from where I stood. "This would be the spot," I said. "If you figure my room was about there," I pointed up, "I guess what was *in* my room would be down here." I waved a hand around, looking down at the mess at our feet.

"We'll need shovels," said Kristy. "I'll go find a couple."

While I waited for her, I thought about what I'd like to find. I pictured my room — and winced. I'd never sleep in my room again. I shook my head, trying to let go of that thought. Then I brought the image back and remembered the things I hoped to find.

My journals. That was number one. I've kept journals ever since I could write, and I've saved them all. I don't write in them every day, but I do record the highs and lows of my life. If I'd lost them, it would be like losing a big piece of my own personal history.

Same with my letters, the ones I kept in the cedar box. Notes from Logan, letters from my grandmother, postcards from friends, birthday cards from my dad. Were they all gone?

Some people don't save things like that. I've seen Dawn throw a letter away after reading it. But me? I'd probably saved every piece of mail I'd ever received. Not every card and letter went into the cedar box, just the most special ones. The ones I particularly wanted to keep safe.

My pictures. Everything from school pictures from every grade to snapshots from vacations with friends and family. My baby pictures. Pictures of my dad when he was a boy.

Pictures of my mom.

I moaned out loud thinking of those. I *had* to find at least one of them. They were more precious to me than anything. Some were ones Mom had kept from her girlhood, some were ones of her and my dad when they were first married, and some had been given to me by my grandmother. She had gone through her collection recently and had sent me most of her pictures of my mom, saying I should have them.

Just then, Kristy returned with two shovels. "What is it?" she asked, seeing my face.

I shook my head. "Just thinking," I muttered.

"Well, there's not much time for that," said Kristy. "Somebody just told us the weather report. It's going to pour tonight."

I looked at her. "So?" I asked. I couldn't think why that mattered.

"So anything that hasn't been pulled out of here is going to be even less salvageable if it rains," she explained. "Your dad's asking people to help move things into the barn. All the stuff out on the lawn, anything else people can grab."

I nodded dumbly.

"People have started bringing tarps by, but

that's not going to be enough," Kristy went on. "We have to cover a big area."

I nodded again.

"But your dad said it's okay for us just to work here for now," Kristy went on. "Stacey and Logan are here, and Claudia's on her way. I think Jessi and Abby will be over later, when the Pikes go home."

"Great," I said. It was nice of my friends to want to help.

"Watson and my mom are heading to the airport soon to pick up Dawn. They wanted to know if you'd like to go with them."

I shook my head. "I want to stay here," I said.

I knew Dawn would be disappointed if I weren't there to meet her, but I hoped she would understand. I just couldn't seem to leave the house, or to stop searching for things I could save.

Kristy and I began to dig through the wreckage, turning over shovelsful of — of what? Ceiling, I suppose, and floor. And pieces of furniture that weren't furniture anymore. The smell was horrendous, and everything we touched was filthy, but we kept on digging until we began to find things that had been in my room.

Kristy found the first item. She held it out on

her shovel for me to see. It was a shoe, or at least it had once been a shoe. Now it was a twisted, blackened piece of leather. But I recognized it as one of my loafers.

Then I found a couple of books. They were charred and soggy, and there was no way I could tell you *which* books they were, but there was no doubt that they were books. I also found one journal, the most recent one. I wasn't sure if I would be able to read it, but finding it made me feel a tiny bit better.

Abby, who joined us later, turned up a very smoky stuffed animal, a pig I'd called Elmer. Jessi found two metal hair clips. And Claudia discovered a partially melted jewelry box, a little heart-shaped tin one that Logan had given me.

By the time it started drizzling we'd filled a couple of cartons with miscellaneous items. It had gotten pretty late. We were lugging them into the barn when Watson drove up in the minivan.

I stood watching as Dawn climbed out, looked at the house, and burst into tears. Then she saw me. She walked to me with her arms wide open, and we hugged. She buried her face in my shoulder and I could feel her sobbing.

But I still didn't cry. I don't know why. I just *couldn't.*

Dawn and I didn't talk then, since it was almost dark and I wanted to keep searching as long as I could. Finally, though, it began to rain for real. Everyone dashed into the barn with one last load of salvage, then raced to cover as much as possible with the tarps.

I gazed back at the house one last time as we left. What a sad-looking wreck. How could we ever rebuild the life we'd had there?

CHAPTER 11

By the time we arrived at Kristy's it was pouring. Rain fell in sheets as we pulled into the garage.

Inside, the house was warm and cozy, and the aromas in the kitchen were delicious. Nannie had been cooking all day, with help from Karen, Andrew, David Michael, and Emily Michelle — who had already eaten, since we were returning so late.

"I peeled the carrots!" David Michael yelled as we walked in.

Karen ran into Kristy's arms. "I stirred the batter for the cake," she said proudly.

"Nannie let me help wash the pots and pans!" claimed Andrew.

Emily Michelle chimed in last. "I mezzer," she told us seriously.

"She helped me measure the flour for a cake," Nannie translated. "And she did a very good job too."

"It smells wonderful in here," said Sharon. "How lovely to come back to a delicious dinner."

"The kids did most of the work," Nannie insisted. "Now, why don't you all go wash up. Take your time — we're in no rush. Then we'll sit down to a nice, calm dinner."

I looked at my dad and Sharon. They were filthy, totally covered in grime. Then I looked down at myself and realized I didn't look much better.

"Clothes!" Watson said, smacking his head. "You'll need clothes."

Kristy's mom spoke up. "All taken care of," she said. "Watson, there's a box out in the van. It's full of clothes that people brought by today. I organized them by size and type, so it should be easy for you all to outfit yourselves."

"I'll get it!" Sam had come into the kitchen as we were talking. He headed for the garage.

Kristy and her family were being so nice to us. How could we ever thank them enough?

Once we'd chosen clothes from the box, Kristy led us upstairs and showed us our rooms. Dawn and I would be sharing the one I'd napped in earlier, and Sharon and my dad would be staying in an even more luxurious room — with its own bathroom — down the hall.

David Michael had followed us up the stairs.

"There's bubble bath in our bathroom," he told Dawn and me. "You can use as much as you want."

"And there are a gazillion towels in this closet," said Karen, who had also trailed after us. She threw open a door to show shelves stacked with piles of clean linens.

We had everything we needed. Dawn and I each took a long shower, then dressed in clean clothes. Dawn had a suitcase full, of course, but I chose from the pile I'd taken out of the box. I pulled on a pair of denim shorts and a yellow shirt that I remembered seeing on Abby. Then we headed down to dinner.

The stew Nannie had made was delicious, but I didn't have much of an appetite. She'd even made a vegetarian version for Sharon and Dawn, but I didn't notice them eating a lot either. I think we were all too exhausted to be hungry.

We were also too tired to talk. The big dining room echoed with chatter, but most of it came from Kristy's family. The kids, who popped in and out while the rest of us ate, were excited to have company. They couldn't wait to show us their rooms. They told us about their pets and how well they were getting along with Tigger. And they asked dozens of questions about the fire, most of which Watson and Kristy's mom tried to answer so we wouldn't have to.

After dinner, our hosts refused to let us help clean up. Dawn and I collapsed in our room. We lay on our beds, fully dressed, and started to talk.

"This has been the strangest day," Dawn mused. "I mean, I was woken up in California when it was still dark out to hear the news about the house. And here I am, in a room at Kristy's. It's, like, how did this happen?"

"I know," I said. "I still can't believe it, even though I spent almost the whole day digging through the rubble."

"Mom looks so tired," Dawn said. Her voice was shaky. "I don't even know what to say to make her feel better." She sniffed a little.

"I know," I said again. "I feel the same way about my dad. It's really hard to see him so upset."

I heard Dawn sniffing again and knew she was crying.

"I feel like the last part of my life in Stoneybrook is over." Dawn sounded miserable. "That house still felt like a home to me. Now I don't even have a real base here. And the things I left behind are probably just — gone."

I knew Dawn had packed up most of her stuff and shipped it to California when she moved there for good. But she'd also left some favorite things so that she'd feel at home when she visited.

I sat on Dawn's bed and put an arm around her shoulders. She began to sob. "I know, I know," I kept saying, the way you'd comfort a child who was weeping. "It'll be okay."

Finally her sobs let up a bit. I gave her one last squeeze and sat back. She looked at me. Her eyes were puffy and her cheeks were stained with tears. "Why aren't you crying?" she asked. Then she sniffed again.

I shook my head. "I don't know. It's strange, isn't it?"

"Strange?" asked Dawn. "It's beyond strange. You *always* cry."

I gave her a faint smile. "Not this time. It's as if — as if the whole thing is just too *big* for me to deal with in my usual way. But I don't know how else to deal with it. I kind of wish I *could* just cry, and then it would be over with."

"I wish you could too." Dawn hugged me again. I haven't felt that close to her in a long, long time.

Just then there was a tap at the door. "It's me," said Kristy. "Can I come in?"

"Sure," we chorused. Dawn wiped her eyes and blew her nose.

Kristy sat on my bed and the three of us talked about what we would do the next day.

In the morning, the Brewer-Thomas household was going full blast by the time Dawn and I came downstairs. David Michael was helping Emily Michelle draw a picture to "cheer up our guests" — and teaching her to sing "Jingle Bells" at the top of her lungs. Karen and Andrew were zooming around the living room, pretending to be firefighters. Nannie was bustling about, making lists of what she had to do that morning while she supervised Sam and Charlie, who were at work making a huge pile of sandwiches for the people who would be helping us at the house. Watson was on the phone straightening out plans with the professional cleaning service we were going to hire for the worst of the job, while Kristy's mom was on another line organizing a "housewares drive" to replace all the kitchen things we'd lost in the fire.

Kristy grinned at us and shouted over the racket, "Welcome to my world!"

She may have been used to that kind of chaos, but I wasn't. And I wasn't in any kind of shape to deal with it. I knew we were lucky to have such a wonderful place to stay and such great friends, but, frankly, if the Brewer-Thomas clan "helped" any more, I was afraid I might not be able to take it. Fortunately, Kristy's mom seemed to understand. She finished one last call, then approached Dawn and me. "I've laid out some breakfast things in the sunroom," she said. "I think you'll find it a little more mellow in there."

Sure enough, the sunroom was a quiet haven. My dad and Sharon were already there, eating breakfast and talking quietly. They stopped suddenly when they saw Dawn and me, and switched to making plans for the day.

Or tried to, between interruptions. First David Michael and Emily Michelle wanted to present us with the picture they'd created. Then Karen and Andrew turned up. They told us they'd made up a play about the brave firefighters to perform for us. Then Nannie popped in to ask what we'd like for dinner. David Michael came back to give us another picture. Kristy showed up to tell us she'd organized the BSC members into two-hour shifts for the day, some working at the house and some volunteering to sit for parents who would be working at the house. David Michael and Emily Michelle burst in partway through her visit to give us a rendition of "Jingle Bells." Sam stopped in to check on whether we'd prefer cheddar or Swiss on our sandwiches.

And so on.

Finally, we finished breakfast and headed over to the house. It was still a shock to see the burned-out shell as we turned into the driveway. "Well, at least the tarps held," my dad said as we climbed out of the car.

We began to strip off the tarps and fold them, since the weather report was calling for a sunny day. As we worked, neighbors and friends arrived and offered help. Jessi arrived with a huge tray of fruit her mom and aunt had put together, and Claudia brought a platter of cookies.

The firefighters had set up a ladder for access to the part of the house that was less burned. They had brought down some salvageable things, such as Dawn's bureau.

Dawn examined it, then jiggled open a drawer. She peered inside. "Wow," she said, with a whistle. "Check it out." She lifted out the top layer of clothing, which was completely blackened with smoke. Then another, lighter gray. And finally a bottom layer that looked almost normal. She held a shirt to her nose. "Stinks, though," she reported.

We worked for hours, digging, carrying, and cleaning. The only high point was when I found my pearl necklace. It used to belong to my mom, and my dad gave it to me on the day he married Sharon. Finding it was a thrill, even though the pearls were covered in soot. But by the end of the day, we didn't have a whole lot else to show for our labors. The fact was, there just wasn't much to save.

I still hadn't found any pictures or letters. And I just kept thinking of more things I'd lost in the fire. Silly things, like my Cam Geary collage, and sad things, like my favorite picture of

Dad and me, the one in which I'm riding on his shoulders (I was two, I think).

I think he felt discouraged too. "Let's call it a day," he said finally, when he and Sharon and Dawn and I gathered beneath the apple tree to compare notes. "I think we all need some rest. Tomorrow morning, when we're feeling a bit better, we'll have a family conference. It's time for us to talk about what happens next."

CHAPTER 12

"No! Don't open that door!" Karen came screeching around the corner just as Sharon was about to usher us into the sunroom. It was Sunday morning, and we'd finished eating the huge pancake breakfast Watson had cooked for us. It was time for our family meeting.

"Why not?" Sharon asked, pausing with her hand on the doorknob.

"Emily Junior's in there," Karen explained. "It's her weekly exercise, when she has time out of her cage."

"Emily Junior?" Sharon asked.

"She's a rat," I whispered.

Sharon jumped away from the door.

"She won't hurt anybody," Karen promised. "You can still go in there. Just be careful not to let her out, or Daddy will be mad."

"She's a pet rat," I explained. "She's really kind of cute."

"Rats are rats," Sharon said firmly. "We'll find another place to meet."

Kristy's house may be enormous, but it was starting to feel like very close quarters. There didn't seem to be anywhere to turn for privacy or quiet time. The sunroom had been our last hope for a meeting place, since every other room in the house seemed to be full of busy, noisy Thomases and Brewers.

Kristy and Watson were in the kitchen, clanging pots and pans around happily as they cleaned up after breakfast.

The dining room was taken by Kristy's mom and Nannie, who were using the big table to organize plates, silverware, blenders, and toasters that had been donated to replace our stuff. Emily Michelle was "hepping" them.

David Michael was in the den, watching cartoons at full volume. Sam and Charlie, who'd slept even later than the rest of us and had missed breakfast, fixed huge bowls of cereal and joined him.

Andrew was sprawled near the bottom of the stairs, playing with his action figures. "Eeeeoowgh!" he narrated loudly as he crashed them into each other. "Wheeooooo!"

I love Kristy's family, but I was beginning to feel a little overwhelmed by them.

I think Sharon and my dad felt the same

way. Dawn too. The four of us stood outside the sunroom, exasperated.

"Should we just use our bedroom?" Sharon asked my dad.

He shook his head. "I'm sure we'll be interrupted there."

"I know," I said. "There's a new playhouse in the backyard. Maybe if we sneak out there quietly, nobody will find us for awhile."

"Fine with me," said Sharon.

"I'm game," said my dad.

I led the way to the playhouse. One by one, we ducked to go through the small door. Inside were four colorful child-sized chairs around a child-sized table. We each took a chair and perched on it. I almost burst out laughing at the sight of my father on his miniature yellow chair. But something stopped me. I guess it was the serious look on his face. He still looked tired too.

"Well," he said, putting his hands on the table. "Here we all are." He gazed around at each of us. "I just want to say how grateful I am that we're all safe and sound."

"I second that motion," said Sharon, reaching out to hold hands with Dawn and me.

"I third it," Dawn added with a smile.

"It's unanimous," I said.

My dad nodded. "It really is the most important thing. I know we're reeling from what's happened, but after all, we still have one another." He paused and looked down at his hands. "That's something that won't change. We're a family, no matter what." He glanced at Sharon. She nodded encouragingly. Dad took a deep breath and went on. "But — "

Just then there was a knock at the door. Dad rolled his eyes. "Who is it?" he called.

"It's me, Kristy. Can I come in?"

Dad sighed. "Sure," he said.

Kristy opened the door and entered. She was carrying a tray loaded with a pitcher and four glasses. "Watson and I saw you head out here. We thought you might like some lemonade," she explained.

"That's very sweet," said Sharon.

"Kind of tart too," said Kristy. "Get it? Tart, like lemons?" She looked around and realized none of us was laughing. "Well, anyway," she said. "I'll just leave this with you." She put the tray down and backed out of the door. "Sorry to interrupt!" she called as she left.

Sharon poured glasses of lemonade and passed them around. "Go on, Richard," she said. "You were in the middle of a thought."

"Right," said my dad. He looked a little uncomfortable, and suddenly I began to wonder just what this family meeting was going to be about.

"You were saying how we'll always be a family," Dawn reminded him. "No matter what."

Dad nodded. "I was about to go on and say that perhaps we should look at this fire as creating an opportunity."

"What?" I asked. "Opportunity? The fire ruined everything." I couldn't believe what I was hearing.

"Let him explain," Sharon said, patting my arm.

Dad cleared his throat. "Sometimes an event like this can open the door to change," he said. "It can be a time to rethink things, to chart new courses."

Dawn looked interested. "What new courses do you have in mind?"

Dad cleared his throat again.

And just then, there was another knock at the door. David Michael stuck his head in. "Watson sent me," he said. "There's a phone call for Mr. Spier. It's from his insurance agent."

My dad let out a sigh. "Can you ask Watson to tell her I'll call back?"

"Sure," said David Michael. He ducked out — then stuck his head back in. "When?" he asked. "When will you call back?"

"Soon." I could tell Dad was making a big effort to sound patient. He checked his watch. "In about an hour."

David Michael gave him the thumbs-up sign and disappeared.

"Dad, what are you talking about?" I asked. I felt my stomach flip over. "Aren't we just going to rebuild the house?" I'd never given a moment's thought to any other plan.

"Let me back up," he said. "First of all, there are a couple of things you should know. For one, Sharon has been feeling very dissatisfied with her job lately."

That wasn't news to me.

"She's even been thinking about a career change," Dad went on.

"Really?" Dawn asked, turning to her mom. "Cool. What do you want to do?"

Sharon smiled. "I'm thinking about architecture," she answered. "Or possibly interior decorating."

"Excellent!" cried Dawn.

"But what does that have to do with the fire?" I asked. "I mean, I think it's great too. You shouldn't have to be unhappy with your job. But what — ?"

"I'm not sure I can find the kind of courses I'd need to take here in Stoneybrook," Sharon explained. "I would probably have to go to a bigger college."

"Like in Stamford?" I asked.

Sharon glanced at my dad.

"Okay, here's the second thing you should

know." Now he was looking me straight in the eye. "Last week I was offered a job. An amazing job. It's an opportunity I never thought I would have."

"But?" I asked. I knew a "but" was coming.

"But it's in Philadelphia."

I was stunned.

"Philadelphia?" repeated Dawn. She looked surprised too. "You mean, in Pennsylvania?"

Dad nodded.

"So you're moving?" she asked.

"*Thinking* about it," my dad corrected her. "Nothing's been decided, nothing at all. It's just something I'd like us all to talk about." He was still looking at me. "Mary Anne? What do you think?"

I shook my head. I was speechless. How could he even consider leaving Stoneybrook? Like me, he'd lived here most of his life. Stoneybrook was home.

"I never thought I'd want to live anywhere but here," he said, as if he were reading my thoughts. "But for a job like this, I would consider it. And Sharon could attend an excellent college."

But what about me? I felt like shouting.

"Last week, when I was offered the job, I thought it was out of the question. But now, after the fire, I'm thinking about it again. Maybe this is a chance for us to start over again."

But I don't want to start over again, I thought. All I wanted was for none of this to have happened. I wanted to be back in my own home, with my own things around me. I wanted to know that life would go on the way it had always gone on.

First my house and most of my possessions had been destroyed. Now my father was talking about moving away from the town where I'd spent my life. "This feels like — like the end of everything," I said finally.

Sharon reached out to touch my hand. "It's not an end," she said. "It's a chance for a beginning."

"Sharon's right," my dad agreed. "This could be the start of a wonderful new life for us."

Dawn was nodding as if she understood.

I sat back in my chair.

Had my whole family gone crazy?

CHAPTER 13

monday

Wow. I'm just — speechles.

I never thouhgt I'd see the day Kristy Thomas would say that!

Oh, ha-ha. Really, though. Wasn't it awesome, what happened today?

Definately. Our charges are the most exellant kids in the univers.

No question about it. I'm all choked up again, just thinking about what they did.

You old softee.

By the time my family meeting ended, Kristy had left the house for a volunteer sitting job with the Rodowsky boys. (Jackie has two brothers: Shea, who's nine, and Archie, who's four.) She knew Claudia was going to be sitting for Matt and Haley Braddock that afternoon, and the two of them had arranged to bring all the kids to the Stoneybrook Elementary School playground. Kristy and Claudia were tired from all the work they'd been doing at my house, so they figured it would be a good idea to take the kids to a place where they'd be able to entertain themselves.

Kristy arrived first, and the boys ran for the playground equipment. Archie grabbed his favorite swing, while Shea and Jackie headed for the jungle gym. They climbed up to the highest bars, calling for Kristy to watch as they swung from bar to bar.

"I'm watching, I'm watching," Kristy called back, wincing as Jackie nearly fell, then caught himself. "Take it easy, Jackie."

Soon, Claudia arrived with Matt and Haley. Haley's a smart nine-year-old who does a great job of interpreting for Matt, who communicates mostly in American Sign Language. (He's the boy who found Jake Kuhn when he was lost.) We've all learned a little ASL (Jessi's actually learned a lot), and Haley is truly fluent.

As they approached Kristy, Matt's hands were flying. "Matt wants to know how Mary Anne is doing," Haley said. "I do too. Is she okay?"

"She's fine," Kristy told them. "Really, she is. I mean, she's upset about her house burning down, but she's not hurt. Not at all."

Haley signed to Matt. He looked relieved.

"But what about her house?" Haley asked. "Where are they going to live?"

"I don't know," Kristy admitted. "I think they're trying to figure that out." At that point, she had no idea what had been said at our family meeting, but she knew something was up. "I wish they'd stay with my family forever, but I doubt that will happen!"

"Is Mary Anne sad?"

That was Jackie. He and his brothers had stopped playing in order to greet Matt and Haley.

Kristy nodded. "Yes, she's very sad. It isn't easy to lose your house and all your things."

Jackie looked somber.

His younger brother, Archie, looked frightened. "Is the fire all out?" he asked.

"Oh, yes!" said Claudia. "The firefighters put it out, Archie. Don't worry about that." She reached out to give him a reassuring hug.

"I keep telling him so," said Shea, "but I guess he doesn't believe me."

"He's just scared," Claudia explained. "It's understandable. Fire is a scary thing."

Kristy and Claudia talked for awhile longer with their charges and promised to take them on a trip to the fire station someday soon. Finally, the kids seemed satisfied with what they'd heard. They ran off to swing and climb, leaving Claudia and Kristy to sit and talk.

"Poor Mary Anne," said Claudia, shaking her head. "She still seems to be in shock."

"I know," said Kristy. "And I don't know what else to do for her. I just want her to know we're all here for her if she needs us."

They sat in silence for awhile. Then Kristy sighed. "I keep thinking about that contest we were going to enter. It would be so great to win! But I've tried and tried to write that essay, and I can't seem to make it work. It has to be in the mail tomorrow."

Claudia gasped. "I almost forgot about that! And I'm sure Mary Anne did. What about the history? Even if you could finish the essay, we'll never pull everything else together in time."

"What essay? In time for what?" Jackie had grown tired of the jungle gym and had reappeared near the bench where Claudia and Kristy were sitting.

"It's for the Baby-sitter of the Year contest," Kristy explained. "You know, the one Charlotte was gathering testimonials for."

114

"Oh, right," said Jackie. "I gave a good one." He smiled proudly.

"You sure did," Kristy agreed. "And we're grateful for it. But if the BSC wants to win this contest, we need more than testimonials."

"What else do you need?" Haley had joined them as well.

"A lot." Kristy groaned. "An essay on why we like baby-sitting, plus a history of our baby-sitting experiences. Mary Anne was supposed to write that."

"So who's going to do it now?" Haley asked.

"Don't look at me," said Claudia. "It would take me a month to do something like that. And the spell checker on my computer would probably blow a fuse."

"I don't think computers have fuses." That was Shea. By now, all the kids had regrouped around Kristy and Claudia.

"Microchip, then. Whatever."

"But the BSC deserves to win the contest!" Haley exclaimed. She looked at Matt, who was signing. "Matt says you guys are the best sitters ever. And we all agree. Isn't there some way we can help?"

Suddenly, Jackie started to jump around. "I know, I know!" he yelled. "We can do it. The kids you sit for!"

"Do what?" asked Kristy, puzzled.

"Write the history of your club!" he said. "I

115

mean, we were there for all of it, weren't we?"

Kristy and Claudia exchanged amused glances. "Well, sure, but — " Kristy began.

"He's right!" Haley said slowly, interrupting. "We *were* there. If all your charges worked together, we could tell the whole story." She looked thoughtful. "When does it have to be done?"

"Tomorrow," Kristy answered.

Haley was taken aback. "Tomorrow?"

Kristy nodded. "So it's nice of you to offer, but obviously there's no way — "

Haley wasn't listening to her. "Okay, here's what we'll do," she said, signing simultaneously so Matt would be in on the plan. "Let's go over to our house. We can use the computer there. . . ."

Haley was on a roll. Claudia and Kristy could only watch openmouthed as she talked.

"We can call the other kids and ask them each to write a part of it. We'll help the ones who are too young to write. Then we can put it all together into one piece. What do you think?" She looked around at the other kids.

"Yea!" they shouted. Matt gave her a big thumbs-up, a sign everyone understood without translation.

"We can do it!" yelled Jackie.

Claudia and Kristy looked at each other and

shrugged. There was no way to stop the kids.

Everyone trooped to the Braddocks' house. Haley called her mom (Mrs. Braddock had brought her cell phone to my house) and explained the situation. When she hung up, she was grinning. "She says it's fine," Haley reported. "She even said she'd type up the final version for us when she comes home. She said the BSC deserves to win."

The kids sat down around the Braddocks' kitchen table and drew up a list of BSC charges. "How about the Pikes?" Haley suggested, noting their names on her pad.

"Definitely," agreed Jackie. "And the Arnold twins."

"Don't forget the Kuhns," said Shea.

Matt finger-spelled a name, and Haley interpreted. "Charlotte? You're right. She'll definitely want to help."

"We'll ask everybody to contribute memories of the BSC," Haley said, scribbling down Charlotte's name. "Once we put it all together, with some help on the details from Claudia and Kristy, it will be a complete history of the BSC." She reached for the phone again and started dialing.

The kids were energized by the project. Claudia and Kristy watched in amazement as they made calls, started up the computer (Matt

117

did that; for a little kid he's a real whiz in that department), and wrote up their own memories.

Before long, the history began to take shape. Shea interviewed Kristy about how the club first began. "I hear you were the one with the big idea," he said, poised to take notes as she answered his questions. "What made you think of a baby-sitting club?"

Kristy told him the story. "Well, one night my mom needed a sitter for David Michael. I remember watching her make all these phone calls, trying to find someone who was free. She was really frustrated. And then it came to me . . ."

Claudia grinned, watching her. Kristy loves to reminisce about the club's beginnings, especially because she plays a starring role. But Kristy's not the only one. All of us enjoy thinking about "great moments in BSC history." That's why it was so much fun for Claud and Kristy to be there while our charges pulled together to put the moments down on paper.

Jackie contributed the story about landing in the hospital after his bike accident and he told how the BSC members rallied around him when he was hurt.

Charlotte came by to bring her contribution, a memory of how the BSC helped her change from a timid, lonely girl to someone with lots of friends.

The Pikes brought over a whole sheaf of written memories, covering everything from talent shows and parades to the time they all had the chicken pox.

The stories flowed in all afternoon, including some that were dictated over the phone. Kristy and Claudia helped a little with organizing the material and typing it into the computer (Kristy did most of that, in order to save the spell checker), but the kids did most of the work. And by the end of the afternoon, the history was done!

And to top it all off, Kristy went home with an excellent idea for her essay.

CHAPTER 14

Why I Like to Baby-sit
by Kristy Thomas
(Note to the judges: This essay should probably have a different title, maybe "Why the BSC Likes to Baby-sit," since it is a group entry.)

Every member of the BSC likes to baby-sit. In fact, we love it. We all like kids and enjoy spending time with them. Children are fun to be around. It's as simple as that.

And it's also a lot more complicated.

Because baby-sitting isn't just about taking care of kids. It's about caring, and community, and connections. I learned a lot about that over the past few days.

Three days ago, my best friend's house burned down. And it was what happened after Mary Anne's house burned down that taught me the real lesson. The one about why I love to baby-sit. First of all, there was the way every member of our club came together to support Mary Anne and to help her and her family. Second was the way that our charges worried about Mary Anne and let her know how much they care. Finally, you may notice that our history section was written by the children we sit for. After the fire, our charges pulled together to make sure our entry was finished on time.

Baby-sitting is a two-way street. We take care of the kids and make sure they enjoy their time with us. In exchange, we receive not just financial rewards but emotional ones as well. Our charges give back every bit of love we show them, and then some.

As I wrote this essay, I came to realize that I don't even care if my club wins the contest. I already know that each and every member of the BSC is the Baby-sitter of the Year—in my heart, in Mary Anne's heart, and in our charges' hearts. That's all the recognition we need.

Kristy put down the paper she'd been reading from. "What do you think?" she asked.

It was Monday evening and we were gathered in Claudia's room for a BSC meeting. I had been planning to skip it, but my dad and Sharon urged Dawn and me to go. "You need some time with your friends," Dad had said. "And some time away from the house." Logan, who had been working with us that afternoon, walked us to Claudia's and stayed for the meeting.

Kristy looked around the room. "Guys?" she asked. "Do you like it?"

Stacey sniffed, then grabbed a tissue from Claudia's bedside table and blew her nose. "Id's beautiful," she said.

"Pass me those, would you?" asked Jessi, who was also sniffing. The tissue box went around the room. Everybody took one, even Logan. Everybody but me.

It wasn't that I didn't like Kristy's essay — I thought it was great. It was well written and very moving. So what was wrong with me? Me, who used to be known as the "Town Crier." I was the only dry-eyed person in the room. This was starting to feel very, very weird. "I love it, Kristy," I said. "If those judges have any sense at all, our entry has to win."

"Thanks, Mary Anne," she replied, giving

me a curious look. I knew she was wondering about the fact that I hadn't been first in line for one of those tissues.

I gave her a half smile. I couldn't explain it to myself, so how could I explain it to her? Logan, sitting next to me, took my hand and squeezed it.

My friends had been wonderful. Their kindness definitely gave me strength. But even with all that love surrounding me, what I mostly felt was — hopelessness. My life had changed overnight. All I could think about was what I'd lost: not just my house but my sense of who I was.

Kristy put her essay aside. "I'll put the whole entry together tonight and send it tomorrow," she promised. She turned to me. "Want to tell us what's going on?" she asked gently.

I shook my head. I wasn't ready to talk about it. "Dawn can tell you."

Everybody focused on Dawn. She looked down at her hands. "It's pretty serious," she said. She took a deep breath. "My mom and Richard are talking about moving away," she said in a rush.

"What?" Kristy cried.

"Away? Like to Stamford or something?" Claudia asked.

Jessi frowned. "They can't do that!"

Logan just squeezed my hand even harder

and looked into my eyes. I looked away.

"It's not for sure," Dawn said. "It's just something they're thinking about. Richard has a job offer in Philadelphia."

"Whoa," said Stacey. "That's pretty far away."

"No kidding," said Kristy. "It might as well be the North Pole. How can they even think about that?" Her face was white.

"They have to do what's right for them," said Dawn softly. "For all of us."

"I can kind of understand," Abby said slowly. "I don't think my family really began to heal from my dad's death until we moved away. Sometimes you have to leave the past behind." Her eyes met mine, and I saw tears in hers.

I sat and listened while my friends discussed my life. I felt detached, as if I were watching a TV show. The things they were saying didn't seem to have anything to do with me. Logan held onto my hand through the meeting, and his touch was the only thing that felt real.

Later, after Kristy had adjourned the meeting, Logan asked if I'd like to take a walk. "My mom will drive you over to Kristy's afterward," he said.

"Go ahead," Dawn urged me. "I'll ride home with Kristy and Abby and see you later."

Logan and I took a long walk together. We

didn't talk much, and we didn't go anywhere near my house. We just held hands and strolled along quietly.

Finally, as we were returning to his house, Logan stopped and looked at me. "Mary Anne," he said, "I'm worried about you."

I looked down at my feet. "I'm okay," I mumbled.

"No, you're not. And that's normal. It would be weird if you *were* totally okay. Something awful just happened to you. What worries me is that you're not talking to anyone about it."

I shrugged. "There's nothing to talk about."

"You know that's not true." Logan put a hand on my shoulder. "Mary Anne, if you can't talk to me, do you think you could talk to Dr. Reese? Maybe it would be a good idea to see her."

Dr. Reese is a therapist I've seen a couple of times in the past, times when I needed someone to talk to about things that were confusing to me. She always made me feel better.

But this time I didn't feel like talking to Dr. Reese, or to Logan, or to anyone. I just wanted to be left alone.

Unfortunately, that wasn't going to happen anytime soon. When Mrs. Bruno dropped me off at Kristy's, I tried to slip up the stairs to my room unnoticed. But David Michael spotted me.

"Mary Anne!" he cried. "Come and see what we're doing." He grabbed my hand and pulled me into the den, where he and Karen and Andrew were making a huge building out of Legos. "Guess what this is?" he asked.

I shook my head. "I don't know."

"It's a new house for you!" David Michael crowed. "We're building the biggest Lego house ever. Do you like it?"

"It's great," I told him. "Thanks." I smiled and edged my way out of the room, only to be greeted by Watson.

"You're just in time for dinner," he announced. "I was about to call the kids. We're having spaghetti with meatballs. Your dad told me that's a favorite of yours."

I wasn't in the least bit hungry, but what could I do? I thanked Watson and headed for the dining room.

Dinner was chaotic, as usual. Emily Michelle dropped a meatball and burst into tears. Sam and Charlie took turns giving play-by-play accounts of that day's baseball game. Kristy kept shooting Looks at my dad, as if that would keep him from deciding to move away. And David Michael and Karen had a noisy, messy spaghetti-slurping contest.

As we were helping to clear the table, my dad pulled me aside. "I know this is hard on you," he said quietly. "Staying here, I mean.

Sharon and I feel the same way. We'll be moving into a rental house as soon as we find one that the insurance money will cover."

That was good news. As much as I loved Kristy, and as much as I appreciated her family's help, we couldn't stay with them forever.

It was time to go.

CHAPTER 15

"Tigger! Tigger! Where are you?"

I could hear him mewing, but I couldn't see him. In fact, I couldn't see much of anything. Smoke filled the room, and flames crackled around me. I stumbled forward, waving my arms in front of me in hopes of touching him.

Finally, I felt fur. "Tigger!" I shouted with relief, scooping him up in my arms. I began to run for the door. But where *was* the door? Even with all the smoke, I should have been able to find it. Somehow, the layout of my room had changed. I felt my way around the walls, wincing as the heat nearly seared my fingertips.

No door. There was no door! Desperate, I ran around the room again. It couldn't be true, but it was. There was no door, no window.

No hope of escape.

Tigger lay quietly in my arms, not struggling at all. He was counting on me to save him. But how could I? I couldn't save myself. I started to pound on the walls, hoping someone would hear. "Help! Help!" I cried as the smoke grew thicker and the flames darted higher.

"Help," I cried one more time, waking myself up.

I lay in bed, my heart pounding. Another nightmare. I'd been having them every single night. Sometimes the fire trapped me in a room; other times I escaped, but only after running down endless unfamiliar hallways.

It was exhausting, having those horrible dreams. When I woke, I was often too wound up to go back to sleep, so I would lie awake for hours, listening to Dawn's gentle breathing from the bed across the room. She wasn't having nightmares. Not that she wasn't upset about the fire — she was. It was just that she hadn't been there, hadn't heard the alarms and smelled the smoke. She was lucky.

She was also lucky because she had another home, back in California. This fire had changed her life, sure — but not the way it had changed mine.

I rolled onto one side and then onto the other. I smushed up my pillow, fluffed it, smushed it again. I tried to imagine myself in a nice, peaceful place. That's what my dad always advised when I was little and couldn't sleep. But the only nice, peaceful place I could picture was my room at home — before the fire. And I didn't want to think about that. It hurt too much.

No matter what I did, I couldn't seem to fall asleep again. And then, suddenly, I didn't want to sleep anymore. I sat up in bed, wide-awake. Then I swung my legs to the floor and stood up. Quietly I rummaged through the pile of clothes at the foot of my bed until I found jeans, sneakers, and a sweatshirt. I pulled on the clothes and let myself out of the room, being careful not to let the door make noise as I closed it behind me.

I tiptoed down the hall, past the room where Sharon and my dad were sleeping. Past Kristy's room, past Sam's. Carefully, carefully, I felt my way down the stairs.

The living room was dark and quiet, with only the light from the VCR blinking at me as I tiptoed by. I moved silently through the kitchen and let myself out the back door and walked to the garage.

An outdoor lamp gave me just enough light to find Kristy's bike, which stood leaning against a row of garbage cans. I put on the helmet that hung from the handlebars.

Okay, let me stop here for just a second and make one thing clear. I know, and I knew then, that going for a bike ride, alone, in the middle of the night, is not a smart thing to do. It's not something I recommend. But I also want to say that I did wear that helmet, and that I made sure the bike had reflectors, and that I was very, very careful to watch out for cars.

I just want to clear that up.

With all this in mind, I walked the bike down the driveway, threw my leg over the bar, and rode off into the darkness.

Where was I going?

To my house. I don't know where the urge came from. It didn't make sense — none at all. But something drew me there, something *deeper* than sense.

I rode through the deserted streets of Stoney-brook, a town I know like the back of my hand. The night was dark and cool and empty, which pretty much describes the way I had been feeling ever since the fire.

There was something peaceful about Stoney-brook at night. The houses I passed were quiet; everyone lay sleeping in their beds. I envied those sleepers as I rode by.

I took a long, meandering route from Kristy's house to mine, letting the bike go where it wanted to. I rode by Stoneybrook Academy, its big old buildings rising high and dark in the night. I rode past the middle school, where one light had been left on in the teach-ers' lounge. I passed the Johanssens' and pictured Charlotte in a deep sleep, then the Ramseys', where Jessi and Becca and Squirt were each tucked into their beds.

I pedaled slowly, feeling the cool night air on my face as I glided past quiet playgrounds with empty swings and baseball diamonds with their ghostly outlines. As I drew nearer to my own neighborhood, each house became even more familiar. I passed Claudia's house, where I've spent so many hours of my life — from babyhood to BSC — and the houses belonging to so many of the charges I've cared for. The Hobarts. The Newtons. The Braddocks. The Kuhns. All children I've come to know and care for, all asleep in their beds.

All the children I would miss so terribly if I moved away.

I let that thought drift off into the night as I rounded another curve and our barn came into view. The barn that was the only thing still standing on our property.

It seemed strange to see the barn standing alone, without a house nearby. I would never grow used to that sight.

Never.

I rode into the driveway and toward the barn. I stopped near the apple tree, got off the bike, and leaned it against the tree trunk. I took off the helmet and hung it on the handlebars.

Then I drew a deep breath and walked toward the barn.

The moon had risen, full and bright, as I rode across town. Now it lit my way as I moved across the yard. I could see the wreckage of my former house almost as well as if it were day. But I knew nothing was there, nothing left to save.

Everything we'd found was in the barn by then. The last pieces of my life, spread out on the dirt floor where horses used to live. I opened the barn door and let it close behind me. Then I began to stroll around, looking at what we'd salvaged. Moonlight poured through the high windows, lighting everything with an eerie glow.

The white bathtub lay gleaming in one corner, a pile of bricks beside it. On top of the bricks were the andirons from our fireplace, decorative wrought-iron ones my dad had bought at an auction.

A jumble of silverware, three blackened pots, and a stainless-steel colander were all that we'd saved from the kitchen.

There was Dawn's small pile, which included a little porcelain dolphin statue she'd always loved. Its nose was broken and the porcelain was stained with soot, but she'd saved it nonetheless. I reached out to touch its cool surface.

My things lay nearby, an odd collection of half-burned objects. They were hardly worth saving, but they were all I had left in the world. I gazed at them: the tin box, the stuffed animal, the blackened pearl necklace, the ruined shoe. I'd found only one picture of my mother. Even her ring on my finger was cold comfort.

Suddenly, there in the cool quiet of the barn, I realized that I'd never felt more alone.

That's when my tears began. And after all that time, they came hard. I cried as I had never cried before, standing amid the few items left from my past. These weren't the kind of tears that fall softly during sad movies, or the kind that slip out during sentimental moments. No, these tears didn't come out of any kind of pleasure or even sadness. These tears were hard and real and they came from pain.

I cried for what seemed like a long, long time. I cried so hard my whole body hurt. I cried so hard I could barely see.

But I noticed when the barn door opened and a light came on.

I noticed when Dawn walked in.

Without a word, she came toward me, arms open. She was crying too. We sank to the floor together to sit and cry some more.

Finally, our sobs slowed. I felt her arm around me and knew that I wasn't alone. Dawn, who had lost *her* house, *her* things, might not have been there for the fire, but she was here now. And there were things she understood. My dad and Sharon understood too. And there were my friends, who were doing their best to help even though they would never truly understand.

"How did you know I was here?" I asked when I could speak again.

"Because I knew this was where I'd want to be," she replied. "I woke up just as you left our room. And when you didn't come back, I realized where you must have gone. I know how it feels. I'm drawn to this place too. Remember, I came all the way from California to be here."

She did understand.

"I — I feel so lost," I said. "It's like I don't know where I belong anymore, or who I am." Still more tears spilled out.

"I know," said Dawn, stroking my hair. "I know."

It felt so good to cry. At last I was *feeling* something, and even though it hurt terribly, it was better than feeling numb. I talked some more, letting everything come out. Everything I hadn't let myself think until now, about my sadness and my fears. Dawn just listened, and comforted me, and let me cry.

We talked about everything that night. About how Dawn would have to go back to California soon, and how my future in Stoneybrook was far from certain. Dawn made me promise that I wouldn't let Sharon and my dad make any decisions without hearing my opinion.

"You know," she pointed out gently, "sometimes good things grow from bad things. Maybe this really is a chance for a new beginning."

I nodded, but I didn't feel the truth of what Dawn was saying. Maybe someday I would. That was something I could hope for. In the meantime, I would have to hang on to what I had. These few sad objects, saved from the fire — and the love of my friends and family. With these things, I would begin a new life.

Dear Reader,

If you have just finished reading this book, then you know about the big change in Mary Anne Spier's life that may be one of the biggest crises any of the BSC members has ever faced. Mary Anne doesn't know where her family is going to live, or even if they're going to stay in Stoneybrook. Her life is going to change . . . and so is the Baby-sitters Club.

Next month will mark the start of the BSC Friends Forever series. The BSC is going to get a whole new look — and a lot of big things are going to happen. I don't want to give away any of the surprises, so keep an eye out for the BSC Friends Forever Special: *Everything Changes*, followed by BSC Friends Forever #1: *Kristy's Big News*. I'm very excited about the new changes and hope you will be too!

Happy reading,

Ann M. Martin

L. GODWIN

Ann M. Martin

About the Author

ANN MATTHEWS MARTIN was born on August 12, 1955. She grew up in Princeton, NJ, with her parents and her younger sister, Jane.

Although Ann used to be a teacher and then an editor of children's books, she's now a full-time writer. She gets ideas for her books from many different places. Some are based on personal experiences. Others are based on childhood memories and feelings. Many are written about contemporary problems or events.

All of Ann's characters, even the members of the Baby-sitters Club, are made up. (So is Stoneybrook.) But many of her characters are based on real people. Sometimes Ann names her characters after people she knows; other times she chooses names she likes.

In addition to the Baby-sitters Club books, Ann Martin has written many other books for children. Her favorite is *Ten Kids, No Pets* because she loves big families and she loves animals. Her favorite Baby-sitters Club book is *Kristy's Big Day*. (By the way, Kristy is her favorite baby-sitter!)

Ann M. Martin now lives in New York with her cats, Gussie, Woody, and Willy. Her hobbies are reading, sewing, and needlework — especially making clothes for children.

Notebook Pages

This Baby-sitters Club book belongs to _____.

I am _____ years old and in the _____

grade.

The name of my school is _____.

I got this BSC book from _____.

I started reading it on _____ and

finished reading it on _____.

The place where I read most of this book is _____.

My favorite part was when _____.

If I could change anything in the story, it might be the part when

_____.

My favorite character in the Baby-sitters Club is _____.

The BSC member I am most like is _____

because _____.

If I could write a Baby-sitters Club book it would be about _____

_____.

#131 The Fire at Mary Anne's House

In *The Fire at Mary Anne's House*, something really awful happens to Mary Anne. When a fire starts at her house, she grabs Tigger and leaves. After the fire is over, she goes through and looks for her journals and other things. The things that are most important to me in my house are _____

_____ because _____

_____. Mary Anne is lucky to have so many friends to help her. Her family even moves into Kristy's house for a time. If I had to live in one of my friends' houses, I would choose _____

_____ because _____

_____. Eventually, Mary Anne's family decides to leave Kristy's. Mr. Spier says they might even move away from Stoneybrook! If I were Mary Anne, I would tell him that I want to _____. The fire at Mary Anne's house is going to bring big changes for her and the BSC. Here are some changes I would like to see: _____

_____

_____.

MARY ANNE'S

Party girl -- age 4

Sitting for the Pikes is always an adventure.

Sitting for Andrea and Jenny Prezzioso -- a quiet moment.

SCRAPBOOK

*Logan and me.
Summer luv at Sea City.*

*My family—
Jeff, Dad and Sharon,
Dawn and me and Tigger.*

Read all the books
about **Mary Anne**
in the Baby-sitters Club series
by Ann M. Martin

Mysteries:

100 (and more)
Reasons to Stay Friends Forever!

More titles... ▶

The Baby-sitters Club titles continued...

☐ MG22881-1	#97	Claudia and the World's Cutest Baby	$3.99
☐ MG22882-X	#98	Dawn and Too Many Sitters	$3.99
☐ MG69205-4	#99	Stacey's Broken Heart	$3.99
☐ MG69206-2	#100	Kristy's Worst Idea	$3.99
☐ MG69207-0	#101	Claudia Kishi, Middle School Dropout	$3.99
☐ MG69208-9	#102	Mary Anne and the Little Princess	$3.99
☐ MG69209-7	#103	Happy Holidays, Jessi	$3.99
☐ MG69210-0	#104	Abby's Twin	$3.99
☐ MG69211-9	#105	Stacey the Math Whiz	$3.99
☐ MG69212-7	#106	Claudia, Queen of the Seventh Grade	$3.99
☐ MG69213-5	#107	Mind Your Own Business, Kristy!	$3.99
☐ MG69214-3	#108	Don't Give Up, Mallory	$3.99
☐ MG69215-1	#109	Mary Anne To the Rescue	$3.99
☐ MG05988-2	#110	Abby the Bad Sport	$3.99
☐ MG05989-0	#111	Stacey's Secret Friend	$3.99
☐ MG05990-4	#112	Kristy and the Sister War	$3.99
☐ MG05911-2	#113	Claudia Makes Up Her Mind	$3.99
☐ MG05911-2	#114	The Secret Life of Mary Anne Spier	$3.99
☐ MG05993-9	#115	Jessi's Big Break	$3.99
☐ MG05994-7	#116	Abby and the Worst Kid Ever	$3.99
☐ MG05995-5	#117	Claudia and the Terrible Truth	$3.99
☐ MG05996-3	#118	Kristy Thomas, Dog Trainer	$3.99
☐ MG05997-1	#119	Stacey's Ex-Boyfriend	$3.99
☐ MG05998-X	#120	Mary Anne and the Playground Fight	$3.99
☐ MG50063-5	#121	Abby in Wonderland	$3.99
☐ MG50064-3	#122	Kristy in Charge	$3.99
☐ MG50174-7	#123	Claudia's Big Party	$3.99
☐ MG50175-5	#124	Stacey McGill...Matchmaker?	$3.99
☐ MG50179-8	#125	Mary Anne In the Middle	$3.99
☐ MG50349-0	#126	The All-New Mallory Pike	$4.50
☐ MG50350-2	#127	Abby's Un-Valentine	$4.50
☐ MG50351-0	#128	Claudia and the Little Liar	$4.50
☐ MG45575-3		Logan's Story Special Edition Readers' Request	$3.25
☐ MG47118-X		Logan Bruno, Boy Baby-sitter Special Edition Readers' Request	$3.50
☐ MG47756-0		Shannon's Story Special Edition	$3.50
☐ MG47686-6		The Baby-sitters Club Guide to Baby-sitting	$3.25
☐ MG47314-X		The Baby-sitters Club Trivia and Puzzle Fun Book	$2.50
☐ MG48400-1		BSC Portrait Collection: Claudia's Book	$3.50
☐ MG22864-1		BSC Portrait Collection: Dawn's Book	$3.50
☐ MG69181-3		BSC Portrait Collection: Kristy's Book	$3.99
☐ MG22865-X		BSC Portrait Collection: Mary Anne's Book	$3.99
☐ MG48399-4		BSC Portrait Collection: Stacey's Book	$3.50
☐ MG92713-2		The Complete Guide to The Baby-sitters Club	$4.95
☐ MG47151-1		The Baby-sitters Club Chain Letter	$14.95
☐ MG48295-5		The Baby-sitters Club Secret Santa	$14.95
☐ MG45074-3		The Baby-sitters Club Notebook	$2.50
☐ MG44783-1		The Baby-sitters Club Postcard Book	$4.95

Available wherever you buy books...or use this order form.

Scholastic Inc., P.O. Box 7502, 2931 E. McCarty Street, Jefferson City, MO 65102

Please send me the books I have checked above. I am enclosing $_____
(please add $2.00 to cover shipping and handling). Send check or money order–
no cash or C.O.D.s please.

Name_____ Birthdate_____

Address _____

City_____ State/Zip _____

BSC998